THE SUPER SHOCKER OF THE WORLD'S FIRST MEGASTORM

IN THE DISASTER AREA...

"The growing network of improvised tunnels in and under the snow is very dangerous for several reasons. First, there is the obvious threat of collapse, burial, and suffocation by mini-avalanches, cave-ins, and the like. More dangerous than the snow, however, are the people. Obviously, law enforcement in such tunnel systems is next to impossible. In many localities, local gangs of looters have established territories. There are reports of deadly inter-gang guerrilla warfare." He set his jaw. "It's kill or be killed."

〰〰〰〰〰〰〰〰〰〰〰〰〰〰〰〰〰〰〰〰

"ALL TOO BELIEVABLE!...
TERRIFYINGLY PLAUSIBLE!...
makes for a satisfying read right down to the last page. Reason: an unguessable surprise ending."
—*Publishers Weekly*

BLIZZARD

George Stone

A Dell Book

For my father, John Timothy Stone,
whose stories of the Great Blizzard of '88
led to the idea for this book.

Published by
DELL PUBLISHING CO., INC.
1 Dag Hammarskjold Plaza
New York, New York 10017

For information contact Grosset & Dunlap Publishers,
51 Madison Avenue,
New York, New York 10010.

Dell ® TM 681510, Dell Publishing Co., Inc.

ISBN: 0-440-11080-7

Reprinted by arrangement with
Grosset & Dunlap Publishers

Printed in the United States of America

First Dell printing—February 1979

Oh! the snow, the beautiful snow,
Filling the sky and the earth below.
Over the house-tops, over the street,
Over the heads of the people you meet,
   Dancing,
   Flirting,
   Skimming along,
Beautiful snow, it can do nothing wrong.
        —John Whittaker Watson,
         "Beautiful Snow"

Prologue

~~~~~~

It was 3:39 P.M. Greenwich Mean Time on May 1 when the observatory at Jodrell Banks confirmed the successful orbiting of the coordinated Soviet satellites, apparently the most recent vehicles in the long-continuing unmanned Cosmos series. The launchings were obviously timed to highlight the exhibitions of military and technological achievement that are an integral part of the annual May Day ceremonies.

American observation satellites had, of course, monitored the operation continuously from time zero, the moment of ignition of the initial launch vehicle, but the British announcement was the first to reach the world press. In a statement released on the morning of May 2, the U.S. National Aeronautics and Space Administration reported that the new satellite launchings were unusual both in number and in relative position. The first had been inserted into a stationary or hovering equatorial orbit over southern Colombia at 72°30′ west, the approximate longitude of Hartford, Connecticut.

More remarkable was the placement of the other six satellites—three each from two separate launch vehicles—in two orbits which intersected at 38° north latitude and 72°30′ west longitude. This was approximately 200 nautical miles east-southeast of Washington, D.C., and due north of the stationary equatorial satellite. In each of these intersecting orbits, the trio of satellites was equally spaced around the earth with orbital velocities adjusted so that one of them passed over the point of intersection every eight hours. Moreover, the two "trains" of satellites were staggered four hours out of phase so that one of the six would cross the intersection every four hours. In concert with the satellite over the equator, they provided the Soviets an extraordinary capability for continuous, tridirectional observation of the western North Atlantic and East Coast of the United States.

A brief announcement the next day from Tass, the official Soviet news agency, mentioned only the equatorial satellite and described it as "an orbital laboratory for atmospheric studies." However, because the intersection of the two multiple orbits lay in a strategically significant location, the principal function of the satellites was generally assumed to be intelligence-gathering.

In late June, a large number of trawlers of the U.S.S.R.'s Atlantic fishing fleet was observed in the same general area—that is, under the May Day intersection. These waters are relatively deep and not considered sufficiently productive to justify large-scale fishing operations. When frequent transmissions be-

8

tween the trawlers and the new satellites began, the Department of Defense ordered constant aerial surveillance and radio monitoring of the "fishing" fleet to supplement existing American satellite coverage. On July 3, two large Russian submarines were detected beneath the surface.

Although U.S. territorial waters were not being violated (the ships were just outside the two-hundred-mile limit) and no international laws or agreements were being broken by this unusual Soviet activity so far as could be detected, concern grew daily within the military intelligence community. One office in the Pentagon was particularly alarmed and leaked to the press a suggestion that the new May Day satellites were "designed to launch and/or guide to targets in the eastern United States orbital and intercontinental missiles carrying multiple, independently targetable thermonuclear warheads."

Senator Earl Reed, Democrat of Louisiana and a senior member of the Armed Services Committee, offered an alternative hypothesis during an appearance on a Sunday interview program. In his opinion, "The Russians are trying to look over or perhaps salvage something from the boats we sank out there last spring." He was referring to the controversial scuttling of obsolete naval vessels which had occurred in that vicinity on April 1.

But neither the Senator's explanation nor the charge from the Pentagon seemed to account fully for the intercommunications and coincident positions of the Soviet ships and satellites.

Increasing anxiety and mounting pressure for action reached a climax when the National Security Council convened on the morning of July 13 at the

9

request of the Chairman of the Joint Chiefs of Staff. On the next morning, *The Washington Post* alleged that the Chairman of the Joint Chiefs had asked the President to: (1) lodge a formal protest with the Soviet government, (2) demand an immediate reduction in the concentration of Soviet ships near the American coast, and (3) demand a full explanation of the functions of the new satellites.

The President rejected these recommendations, according to *The Post*, on the grounds that there existed only unsupported suspicions and that the concerns expressed had been discounted by a majority of his closest military and foreign-policy advisors. It was generally concluded that, without hard evidence of operations directly imperiling the national security, the Administration was reluctant to provoke any sort of confrontation that could prove detrimental to the professed spirit of cooperation between the two superpowers.

Two days later, the level of Soviet activity began a steady decline. By July 31, all Russian submarines had departed the area, and a few days later the trawlers started to disperse in small groups. On August 20, White House Press Secretary Dan Simon announced that no foreign ships remained in the vicinity and that aerial surveillance had already been discontinued.

Interest in the forthcoming off-year elections was rising, and domestic politics soon dominated the news in Washington once again. The Russian satellites which had attracted so much attention earlier in the summer had been more or less accepted as primarily intelligence-gathering devices after all. (Hardly anyone, of course, had believed the standard Kremlin explanation that their sole purpose was nonmilitary scientific research.) By election day in November, memory of the incident in July had faded from the public consciousness.

1

~~~~~~

WASHINGTON NATIONAL AIRPORT:
  3:00 PM, WEDNESDAY, DECEMBER 20

TEMPERATURE: 34°F

BAROMETER: 29.96″ (RISING)

WIND NW 5–7 MPH

PRECIPITATION: NONE

FORECAST: CLEARING AND COLDER
TONIGHT, INCREASING CLOUDINESS WITH
A CHANCE OF SNOW FLURRIES TOMORROW

John Conroy glanced around the front of the nursery.
An inch of fresh snow decorated the dead grass.
Christmas trees were propped in disorderly rows,

leaning against board railings like the ranks of a drunken army. A gravel driveway clogged by customers' cars led to the office and greenhouses in back. Conroy walked down the driveway and angled left into an aisle between two rows of evergreens. A man stepped out in front of him. "You want tree, mister?"

Startled, Conroy nodded, "Yes."

"What kind? Scotch pine, fir?"

"Scotch pine."

"Big, middle, or little?" the short, swarthy man was wearing a navy-blue pea coat and skullcap. He had a heavy black mustache and fierce black-brown eyes. Conroy guessed he was Greek.

"Uh, middle."

"Okay. Next row, far side. Best trees in Bethesda. You go look." The man pointed with a black glove.

"Thanks." Conroy followed a cross path into the next aisle. He inspected the ranks carefully, pausing to scrutinize each individual pine. He stared, unable to concentrate. At length he lifted one out and rotated it. Full and symmetrical, but a little short. A shower of loose snow fell from its branches, dusting his pants and the tops of his boots. He looked up at the sky, letting the tree fall back into its slot against the rail. Low clouds breaking up. White and blue.

Conroy turned back the end of his glove to see his watch: 3:46 WED 20. He was to have reported for emergency duty on the project at noon. Hell, Berger'll manage in my absence—he's been pushing to take over anyway. He follows orders and loves to give them. Just right for Admiral Zimber: ambitious and unprincipled. Conroy worked a pack of cigarettes from the pocket of his faded trenchcoat. He was tall

14

and slender with slightly stooped shoulders. Straight brown hair drooped over his forehead. His thin face looked pale and tired, older than its thirty-six years. Zimber didn't give a damn about my quitting yesterday. Those phone calls last night and this morning. All that bullshit about my being indispensable. Conroy lit a cigarette and exhaled a cloud of smoke. The implied threats told the story. Zimber's afraid I'll blow the whistle.

He looked up at the sky again. I shouldn't've lost my temper . . . asking for trouble. Paul Garfield was right. I should've followed his example and gotten out long ago. Maybe Jane and I should leave town for a while. Go to New York for the holidays. We could get together with Garfield. No . . . she likes Christmas at home. Oh, well. He took another drag. At least it's better to be outside buying a tree than buried in project headquarters.

He walked a little farther down the line and stopped before another tree. This one looks good. Probably too tall for Jane, though. She likes 'em shorter. Or fuller. They're never quite right. Conroy always shopped for Christmas trees alone—and knew that he wouldn't find the right one. With a child they would all have gone together, and any tree would have been a joy. Hell. He grabbed the tree in the middle of its trunk and wheeled around.

"You like that tree, mister?" The Greek.

"It'll do. How much?"

"Twenty-two dollar."

"Jesus. . . . Okay, here." He handed him two twenties.

"I get you change."

"Uh . . . look, I'll take it to my car."

15

"I take it for you."

"No, that's all right. Go ring it up."

"Okay, mister. Where you parked?"

"Around the corner." He pointed. "Half a block down. Ford wagon."

"Meet you there." The Greek slipped out of sight.

"A blue van was double-parked next to the car. Its back doors were open. Two men were standing there talking, preparing to load several trees. Conroy propped his tree against the tailgate and reached for his keys. He was getting hungry, thinking about dinner. I'll stop on the way home and pick up some wine for tonight. Hell, why not go out? Be good for us to live it up and relax for a change.

"Help you with your tree buddy?" one of the men asked.

"No, thanks."

"Here's change, mister." The Greek's voice was behind him.

"That was fast." As Conroy turned, one of the men by the van raised a dark object and hammered it across the back of Conroy's head. But the blow had not landed solidly. Conroy grunted, "Oh, Jesus," and staggered forward. When he looked around to find his attacker, the blackjack smashed into his face, cracking the cheekbone. His mind flashed red, then black. He slumped into the arms of the Greek. One of the others lifted Conroy's legs as the third placed a Christmas tree on top of him. The three quickly shoved man and trees into the open van. The Greek and the man with the blackjack jumped in behind. Conroy's Chow Chow was barking furiously inside the closed wagon as the van lurched forward and accelerated down the street.

The driver glanced into the back. "Got any idea who this guy is?"

The man with the blackjack was taking something from a canvas satchel. "No more than you: his address, his car, his photograph." The speaker was tall and muscular, his face tight and expressionless. He opened a small leather box and extracted a hypodermic. "The contract came outa Baltimore. As long as the other half of the fee is paid, I don't wanna know." His lips barely parted as he spoke, like a ventriloquist. He snapped a needle to the end of the syringe.

"What you give him?" asked the Greek.

"Air."

"Crazy thing." The Greek pulled off his cap and scratched his bald scalp.

"What's that?"

"Air in lungs is life. Air in veins is death."

"Uh-huh." The tall man pushed the long steel needle into the side of John Conroy's neck.

"You learn that in CIA?" The Greek watched the plunger. The other didn't answer. "Who takes body when we leave in garage?"

"That's not for us to know either." He pulled out the needle, puckering the skin. "But he'll probably go to the funeral home."

"Which one is it?" the driver asked.

"Some place in Baltimore." He put the hypodermic box back in the satchel.

"They bury him?" wondered the Greek.

"No. Crematorium. Here, gimme a hand."

"Ahh . . . oven!" The Greek lifted the legs as they lowered Conroy into a trunk.

17

2

~~~~~~

MANHATTAN, ROCKEFELLER CENTER: WEDNESDAY, DECEMBER 20

TEMPERATURE: 29°F

BAROMETER: 30.11" (RISING)

WIND: NW 8–10 MPH

PRECIPITATION: NONE

FORECAST: CLEAR AND COLD TONIGHT, INCREASING CLOUDINESS AND A LITTLE WARMER TOMORROW

Paul Garfield opened the oven and lifted out a well-baked cherry pie. Hot red juices were bubbling up through slits cut in the crust. He placed it on the counter to cool, then took a loaf of wheat-germ bread from the refrigerator. After untwisting the tie and opening the plastic bag, he pulled out two crumbly slices. A small piece broke off and fell to the counter top. The morsel rolled a few inches and wobbled to rest. Instantly it was seized by the hooked beak of a swooping pea-green marauder. The parakeet streaked out of the kitchen and banked left into the living room with a screeching chirp of triumph. Its wings rose and fluttered as it settled onto a gangling spider plant suspended from the ceiling near the front windows.

"War Eagle strikes again," Paul smiled to himself as he ripped a crisp leaf of lettuce from the head. Next, a pile of sliced ham and too much Dijon mustard. He patted the protesting sandwich on a plate, holding it together as he cut it roughly in half. Wiping his hand on his jeans, he glanced up at the wall clock—10:23—then picked up the plate and followed the bird into the living room.

Paul appeared shorter than he was—an even six feet—because of the breadth of his shoulders and well-muscled body. An athlete in high school and college, he had kept himself in good condition through his twenties by running and swimming. But now at thirty-five, he exercised less, smoked more, and was beginning to accumulate a thin layer of fat. His handsome, almost square face had filled out slightly to a boyish roundness. The naturally intense expression had softened and flashed easily into a captivating smile of playful blue eyes, proud white teeth, and unruly straw-blond hair.

The living room smelled of cigarette smoke. On the coffee table were two stacks of blue booklets, a full

19

ash tray, and an open can of beer. Paul swung his stocking feet up on the couch and took a big bite of sandwich. He peered at the bird, who had dropped his bread on the carpet and was looking toward the windows and the night lights of Manhattan beyond. "Poquito, you're a pig," Paul announced through a mouthful of sandwich. A glob of mustard dropped onto his beige crew-neck sweater. Poquito swiveled his head with a sharp chirp of indignation. The telephone rang. "Goddamm it!" Paul put down the sandwich and reached to the floor for the phone. "Hello."

"Hi, Paul. It's Howard," proclaimed Paul's colleague on the faculty at Columbia. The bird heard Howard Tannenbaum's loud voice and cocked its head.

"Oh, hi Howard, I thought it might be a student. How's by you?"

"Great. Just finished my last grades and gettin' ready for the weekend. You done?"

"Nope. I got tied up this afternoon. Looks like an all-nighter with my undergrad exams."

"What happened? Shack up with Barbara?"

"No such luck. I had some crap to get done at the office."

"Still think you can get away by afternoon?"

"Hope so. I'll call you in the morning." Paul moistened the corner of a handkerchief with beer and attempted to remove the mustard stain from his sweater.

"I just caught the weather and ski report. That snow flurry last night dumped a foot in Vermont. Should be great. I was just down in the garage and got the snowmobile and skis in the truck ready to go."

"What's the forecast for tomorrow?" The stain was blending into the sweater.

"Um, there's another small storm comin' across Carolina, but we shouldn't get anything."

"Sounds good, Howard. I know you're excited, but the best thing I can do is get to work. I'll call before noon."

"Okay, baby. Do your best. Just so we can get started before the rush. Later." They hung up.

The parakeet added his farewell chirp and flew to a rubber tree in the corner. Paul watched him. "Poqui, you'll have to hold the fort for a few days." The bird turned its head, then abruptly flitted over to light on his shoulder. "Oh, you'd rather go skiing?" Paul held out his index finger, and the parakeet jumped on. "Sorry, friend. Too cold and too much snow up there. You'd be buried and freeze." As Paul leaned forward to take another bite of sandwich, the bird hopped to his head and began grooming the tangled hair. At the sound of the phone he darted back to the rubber tree. "Oh, hell. You get it, bird. Then leave it off the hook. . . . Hello."

Dong, dong, dong, ding! Coins in a pay phone. "Paul?"

"Yes?"

"It's Jane Conroy."

"Jane! How the hell are you? What's the occasion?" Paul put down his sandwich and pulled out a cigarette.

"I'm fair. I need to see you tomorrow."

Paul lit up and whistled out a stream of smoke. "Sure. Where are you? Are you home?"

"I'm in a phone booth."

"I heard. I mean, are you in Bethesda?"

"Yes. Would noon be okay?"

"Uh . . . sure. Are you coming to New York?"

"Yes. Yes, I guess so. Let's—"

"Is John coming?"

"No—I don't know."

"What's wrong, Jane? You sound—"

"I can't talk, Paul. Let's meet at twelve-thirty where we used to go for beer."

"You mean—"

"Don't say it! You know where. The old regular place at twelve-thirty. Okay?"

"Okay, but . . . can't you tell me what it's about?"

"No, I'd better not. Tomorrow. But it is urgent—an emergency."

"Is there anything I can do tonight?"

"No. Thanks, Paul. If there's a change, I'll call. "Bye." Mmmmmmmmmm. Dial tone. Paul slowly replaced the receiver as Poquito flew back to his shoulder.

The fire ignited, streaming smoke flashed into flames. They grew rapidly, reaching for the chimney. "Good fire, Wong. Plenty of reach." Curtis Zimber crossed his bare feet on the footstool in front of the stone fireplace. Above the mantel arched a five-foot barracuda.

"Thank you, sir. I shall get you your nightcap." The uniformed houseman hurried out of the Admiral's large study.

Admiral Zimber glanced at his wrist watch. Five after eleven. He sighed and clasped his hands behind his head, staring at the pulsating flames. He had been a fire-watcher most of his life. The fascination had first come when he was a small boy, camping in the north woods with his father. He found the fire trance both relaxing and conducive to clear thought. His father had called it an oriental element: calming in its power, mystery, and immortality.

The Admiral was relatively short and quite stout. The mound of his stomach rose and fell with his breathing. In spite of his heaviness—or, perhaps, because of it—he appeared robust and in good health for fifty-eight. The hair around the sides of his head was a lustrous dark brown; scattered strands lay across the balding crown.

The houseman re-entered the room carrying a tray. He carefully placed it on the table next to the Admiral's leather easy chair. "Shall I pour it for you, sir?" He waited several seconds for a reply. The flames reflected from his glistening black eyes. The redwood-paneled room was lighted only by the fire and the table lamp at the Admiral's side.

At length the Admiral looked up. "Oh, yes. Thank you, Wong." Again he looked at his watch.

"Are you thinking about your meeting with the President tomorrow?" Wong poured a shot glass of bourbon into a steaming cup of coffee.

"Yes." Admiral Zimber grunted and pushed himself to his feet. "The President and the Secretary of Defense. It's not a convenient time for me . . . enough other things to worry about." He stepped into his slippers. "They could've waited until after the holidays."

"What do they want, may I ask?" The houseman backed out of the way as the Admiral started across the room with the coffee cup.

"Oh, I've got to reassure them about development

23

of the drone submarine." Zimber's jaws sagged into an ugly scowl. "Fuckin' Senate subcommittee's been making a lotta noise." He turned on a floor lamp next to a large table. On top of a bookcase to the left stood a perfect scale model of the American clipper ship Flying Cloud (built in 1851). "President shouldn't be any problem, though. Been there before." He put down his drink and spread out several large papers. "Is Mrs. Zimber asleep yet?" The Admiral smoothed a map of some islands in the Bahamas and placed beanbag paperweights on its corners.

Wong approached the table. "No, sir. I think she is still watching television."

"Drinking?"

"Yes, sir. I believe so." He leaned forward. "Which one is your island?"

Zimber thrust a stubby finger to the map. "This one. New Georgia."

"Like in the Solomons?"

"That's where the Japs killed my twin brother, Martin." He nodded and swallowed some of the spiked coffee.

"Where will the house be?"

"North end. On the side of this little bay. We can dock Mariah there. Here, have a look at the plans." He pulled over a set of blueprints. "Twenty thousand square feet—counting the porches." He looked up. "Nothin' like that on Taiwan, is there?"

"Well, not many. When will construction begin?"

"Already has. We've only got a year and a half now."

"You must be very—" The telephone rang. "Shall I answer it, sir?" Wong moved toward the phone.

"Which line is it?" Zimber checked his watch.

"Special security."

"I'll get it." The Admiral hurried to his desk and grasped the phone. "Zimber."

"Good evening, Admiral." It was the voice of Walter Popowski, Zimber's Civilian Assistant for Special Projects.

"Yes, Walter. What's the report?"

"Everything's go. So far, so good."

"And security?"

"All contractual obligations have been met."

"No problems?" Zimber sank into his swivel chair.

"None. Something else, though."

"Like what?"

"Our Columbia alumnus got a call from the wife. They've got a date tomorrow."

"Oh? . . . I didn't think there was any contact there. . . . Well, it may be harmless. Continue monitoring and initiate surveillance."

"Done. See you in the morning."

"Oh eight hundred. 'Night." Zimber hung up and leaned back. "Freshen up my coffee, will you, Wong?"

"Yes, sir." He picked up cup and tray and quickly left the room. Once again Admiral Zimber was staring into the flames.

3

〜〜〜〜〜〜〜〜〜〜〜〜〜〜〜〜〜〜〜〜〜〜

WASHINGTON NATIONAL AIRPORT:
10:00 AM, THURSDAY, DECEMBER 21

TEMPERATURE: 31°F

BAROMETER: 29.89″ (FALLING)

WIND: E 12–17 MPH

PRECIPITATION: NONE

FORECAST: MOSTLY CLOUDY WITH
OCCASIONAL SNOW FLURRIES TODAY,
CLEARING AND COLD TONIGHT

"Well, I guess things will be a lot quieter on the Armed Services Committee next year." Joni Dubin paused, hoping for a response. Senator David Bradford was standing behind his office desk sorting papers into two piles. His large frame was unobtrusive in well-tailored brown herringbone, but the youthful Senator's presence was nonetheless imposing. His dignified, controlled manner elicited confidence and respect. Yet the obvious intelligence and sincerity were blended with natural warmth and charm that put one at ease. And a sense of fun seemed always ready to spring forth from just below the surface—especially for old and close friends like Joni Dubin.

"I mean," Joni continued, "the R and D Subcommittee has completed your 'funny-money' investigation, hasn't it? There's no chance it'll be resumed next Congress, is there?" Another pause. "Well, am I right?"

Without looking up, the Senator replied, " 'Terminated' is the word, not 'completed.' "

"Are you going to do any more?"

"Perhaps." He was still sorting.

Crossing her legs, Joni gazed at the ceiling in a cutely inquisitive pose and cautiously pursued her point. "You're really on to something, aren't you?"

Suddenly she had the full attention of the Senator's deep-brown eyes, the strong handsome face. He watched her in silence, weighing his response. Joni Dubin seemed even more beautiful and appealing than when they had first known each other in Denver ten years before. Straight black hair hung loosely on her shoulders, framing a bright sensitive face of marble-smooth skin. She was wearing a navy-blue suit and powder-blue turtleneck. Her entire mien bespoke competence and professionalism. Their carreers had brought both of them from Colorado to Washington,

D.C., where Joni was now a free-lance television correspondent. David Bradford smiled and put his hands on his hips. "There's no use trying to con you, is there, Miss Dubin?" he asked with sham formality.

"I thought so. You've been impossible to get hold of lately." She uncrossed her legs and leaned forward. "But if you do have something, maybe you'll be able to get the inquiry reopened."

He shrugged, looking toward the window. "Not unless I can get enough evidence to use you—the press—as a lever."

"How can you do that without the budget and staff?"

"Just scratch along on my own. Frank will be helping me full-time during the break." Frank Taylor was a law student serving as Senator Bradford's part-time assistant.

"How is he? I haven't seen him for a while."

"He's fine. He should be here in a few minutes."

"Well, if the subcommittee was willing to support the inquiry in the first place, why won't they carry it through?"

"Because it's been eyewash from the start." He sighed and turned back to face her. "Just going through the motions to avoid charges of coverup. Same old story. Basically, no one cares enough to upset 'business as usual.' The Defense budget's always been full of inflated and misrepresented items. It gives people over there a lot of money to play with under cover—and the sanctity of national security. Money means power, buys friends and influence. Military porkbarrel. Somebody's always hollering waste and secrecy, but nothing changes. Like tax reform."

"So what makes you think you'll get anywhere?" Joni's eyebrows arched. "Are you still after that drone-submarine project?"

"Yes. That's one of the most blatant examples. We're finding some pretty outrageous stuff."

"What's the name of the Admiral who's pushing it?"

"Curtis Zimber. He's extremely powerful—and completely unscrupulous. His type is dangerous."

" 'Outrageous' is pretty strong."

"Used to be one of your favorite words." He smiled softly.

"Still is." She looked down at the antique-gold carpeting. "Come on, stop trying to change the subject." Her large blue eyes looked up again, "What's outrageous? What are you tracking?"

"Do me a favor, Joni?"

"Keep this off the record?"

"Absolutely confidential."

"Of course," Joni sucked in her lips in symbolic pledge.

Staring at the top of his massive mahogany desk, the Senator continued almost inaudibly. "Remember the Lockheed and CIA payoff scandals?"

"Go on."

"And the South Koreans buying Congressmen?"

"Jesus," she whispered, her forehead tightened into a vertical crease.

"It's in that ball park."

"In Congress?"

"Maybe. I'm not sure there. But elsewhere almost certainly."

"Pentagon?"

"Uh-huh."

"Good God, David. No wonder—" The intercom buzzed.

"That's all I dare say now. I'm telling you because I may need your help if it proves out." He reached for the intercom switch. "Yes, Marian?"

"Frank's here, Senator," advised a mellow female voice. "He has your car ready."

"Okay. Please ask him to wait a few minutes. Thank you."

"You *are* leaving early." Joni took a small clipboard from her shoulder bag.

"Between you and me, I'd rather work all day, but Carla wants me to help her finish our Christmas shopping."

"That's how I'll spend my afternoon too."

"Which reminds me," he smiled into Joni's eyes, "I'll have to sneak off and get your present." He walked over to a table near the side windows. "I promised to pick Carla up before lunch and spend the afternoon with her . . . getting exhausted. I hoped we'd at least have a good day for it," he was looking out at the gray sky, "but I see it's turned cloudy."

"And chilly. Feels like it wants to snow."

"I wouldn't mind some more. That's one of the things I miss most in Washington." He pulled the little envelope from a tea bag. "Not much real winter." Joni watched him pouring hot water. "May I fix you some tea or coffee?" he asked.

"No, thank you."

The Senator returned to his desk with a steaming cup. He glanced at the digital clock: 10:50. "I guess I'd better think about going." He put down his tea and spread both hands flat on the desk top, leaning

30

forward in a sort of relaxed bulldog stance. "What else is it you've been wanting to see me about?" He eyed her clipboard. "Must've been more than a few questions about the end of the investigation."

"You mean in addition to your body?" she teased.

"Careful. This place may be bugged." He was giving her his askance glance of mock disapproval. "As a matter of fact, I know it isn't—just had it checked again. Come on, Frank's waiting."

"I want to tape a series of interviews with you to be telecast right after the convening of the new Congress." Her hands curled up in tight fists on her knees.

"For Public Television?" He was pleased.

"Maybe—don't be greedy. Denver for sure, and almost certain statewide syndication. If it's good, PBS may use parts in a special on changes in the Senate. Now, I have four ten-minute segments planned." She swallowed; a slight blush of excitement had come into her cheeks. "The first one, of course, will focus on the early years: growing up and highlights of your skiing career, reaching a climax with the Olympics. Second," her voice was increasing in speed and volume, "law school, practicing in Denver, and election to the Colorado House. Next—"

"Wait a minute. Slow down." He held up his hand in traffic-cop fashion. "It sounds like you're talking about a major project. As I've told you, this is a busy time. I can't promise much time before the opening session."

"You won't have to. Most of the background work is done." She smiled. "I'm well prepared, you know. I figure all I'll need from you is two or three one-hour sessions." He returned her grin and rubbed his hands together. "Now," she continued, raising her pen for emphasis, "let me complete my outline so you'll have the whole idea."

"Okay." He folded his arms across his chest, watching her with more than professional interest.

"The third installment will review your two terms in the House, with special attention to your key role in the Judiciary hearings. And finally," she beamed, "your appointment and subsequent election to the United States Senate."

She continued with somewhat less emotion, "It would not be at all original simply to point out the similarities of your achievements as the first Black to excel in skiing and the first Black Senator from 'Middle America.' I intend to probe much more deeply than that."

"Speaking of 'probe,'" he grinned, "be sure to mention your campaign bumper sticker: 'Ski Bradford'—and the variations thereof."

"I'll never live that down. Those damn jokes," she muttered. "'Pole on Bradford'; 'Take him from the top.'" Joni adjusted her posterior on the chair. "Now, be serious, David. I want to give the viewers a realistic appreciation of the barriers in both skiing and politics and of the ways in which you overcame them. Then we'll do a little speculating about the effects of all this on you and your future."

"You know, modesty usually prevents me from speculating." He cleared his throat exaggeratedly.

"Oh yes, of course." She stood up, tall and trim. "Are there any times soon when we could get together?"

"It's really hectic for me till Christmas." Tightening his brown-and-cream-striped tie, "How about the in-between week—before New Year's?"

"Fine. Any particular days?"

"Christmas is Monday. Could we . . . tell you what, call me Tuesday. I'll know my schedule by then." He smiled warmly. "You wouldn't be laying groundwork for your book idea with these interviews?"

"Got any other commitments?"

"Couple of feelers is all."

"Well, then," seizing her chance, "I'm delighted to accept your proposition. Let's start planning for it." He was shaking his head and chuckling to himself as he moved back behind the desk.

"Oh, David."

"Hmmmm?"

"Would you phone me instead? Carla *was* pretty cool the last time I called."

He grinned and nodded. "Okay. Late morning?"

"Fine."

He pressed the intercom button.

"Yes, Senator?"

"Marian, please ask Frank to come in now."

"Yes, sir."

Again facing Joni, "Speaking of the old days, what do you hear from Paul?"

"Not much. We had lunch in New York a couple of months ago."

"He still want to remarry you?"

"No. I think he's finally adjusted."

The main door of the paneled office opened, and in strode a tall young man wearing a green denim suit. "Hi, Joni. How's the television business?"

"Hi, yourself. It's lookin' up. Got a hot subject

here," glancing at Senator Bradford, then biting her lip. "Uh, how's law school going?"

"Great! Really great." He smiled, adjusting his horn-rimmed glasses. "It's really demanding, but I love it."

"That's wonderful. I'd like to hear about it. Let's get together for coffee or lunch sometime soon."

"Great!"

Joni glanced at her watch. "Look, I've got to run. Good to see you, Frank. Take care. And thank you *very* much, Senator."

"You're most welcome, as always." He helped her with her coat and shoulder bag. "I'll talk to you Tuesday. Have a merry Christmas."

"The same to you both, and thanks again." Frank opened the door, and, with a final wave, she was gone.

He turned to the Senator. "She's really great."

"Yes. I wish there were more like her." They walked over to the desk. "Frank, let's take the right-hand stack and that mixed pile in front."

"Yes, sir. The car's outside as you requested." Frank started organizing papers in a portable filing box.

A steady breeze from the northeast was chilling under low gray overcast. The air smelled like snow. Senator Bradford watched as Frank placed a file box and large briefcase into the trunk of the ivory sedan. When he closed it and took out the keys, the Senator extended his hand. "Come on, my turn to drive."

"Yes, sir. May I ride in back?"

Senator Bradford grinned. "Get in there in front and remember your place. Come to think of it, it might be safer in back."

They pulled away from the Dirksen Senate Office

34

Building and drove around Union Station, continuing northwest on Massachusetts Avenue. "Frank, see if you can get a weather report. I'm supposed to be driving around all afternoon."

After checking his watch, Frank dialed a continuous-news station. Editorial comments regarding the latest construction halt on extensions of the Metro subway system were just concluding. Then, in an annoyingly cheerful voice, "Well, folks, I guess we'll be deluged by the usual irate letters and phone calls from you Christmas shoppers. The weather just isn't cooperating this Thursday, December twenty-first.

"We have been predicting mostly cloudy skies with occasional snow flurries for today, followed by clearing tonight. But now it looks as though we may get a little more snow than we bargained for. The weak storm that's bringing the precipitation has moved out over the Atlantic and is showing some signs of slowing down and intensifying." Scattered snowflakes appeared in the air as Senator Bradford's car rounded Scott Circle and turned north on 16th Street. "So, we're real sorry, but we've had to revise our fearless forecast, good buddies."

That guy's a real asshole," mumbled Frank, earning a mild frown from David Bradford.

". . . one to three inches this afternoon and early evening. So be sure to bundle up those kiddies if you plan to venture into the great out-of-doors."

"I guess you're right," the Senator reconsidered.

". . . already started snowing in downtown Baltimore, so it may begin in the District any time now. Snow has also been reported as far north as Boston, and there is light rain in New York City. Streets may become slick this afternoon, so please drive carefully. Now for a look . . ."

"I've heard enough. Thanks, Frank." Off went the radio. "You never know about snow flurries. Remember the ten inches of 'snow flurries' we had last February?"

"I sure do. I missed classes that day. Oh well, maybe we'll have a white Christmas. So to speak."

By the time they pulled into the driveway of the Bradfords' two-story brick house, the snow was falling thickly. A large feathery flake flew directly into the Senator's eye as he stepped from the car. Reaching for his handkerchief, he squinted up at the cloud-laden sky.

4

〜〜〜〜〜〜〜〜〜〜〜〜〜〜〜〜〜〜〜〜〜〜〜〜〜〜

MANHATTAN, ROCKEFELLER CENTER:
NOON, THURSDAY, DECEMBER 21

TEMPERATURE: 37°F

BAROMETER: 29.93″ (FALLING)

WIND: SE 11–18 MPH

PRECIPITATION: LIGHT RAIN

FORECAST: RAIN ENDING BY EVENING,
CLEARING AND COLDER TONIGHT

DON'T WALK DON'T WALK commanded mercurochrome red. Paul Garfield obediently stopped to wait for the traffic light. Staring downward, he noticed his shoes; water soaking up from the soles was darkening the orange-brown leather. His socks suddenly felt wet and caused him to shudder in the piercing wind. It had been raining in New York for almost two hours. His watch showed 12:21. A pleasant early morning had become a very unpleasant afternoon: gray and wet and raw. WALK ordered emerald green.

Looking to his left as he crossed Third Avenue, he spied several policemen standing under the red-and-white canopy of Tuesday's Restaurant. Wonder what they're doing, what happened . . . maybe a holdup. He squinted. Funny, no police cars.

Heavy noise at the right! His head swiveled. Lurching dump truck. Splashing water. Paul leaped back reflexively as the massive vehicle pounded by. Less than two seconds.

He shook his head and puffed from full cheeks as if expelling fright. His pulse was fast and loud in his ears. That driver had been hurrying to turn before the light changed and assumed he'd get the right of way. He did too. Paul twirled the handle of his black umbrella as he walked slowly westward. It was the second time in an hour he'd narrowly avoided an accident. He'd better keep his mind in the real world. Watching for traffic, he angled right to the north side of 18th Street.

The temperature seemed lower. The wind at his back was driving a cold, stinging rain. He pulled up the fur collar of his topcoat; its softness felt good against his neck. Approaching Irving Place, he was pleased to see the brick-red walls and black trim of his destination. Wonder if Jane's there yet. He turned right, paused under the awning to collapse his umbrella, then pulled open the double doors to enter Pete's Tavern.

It was a comfortable place for relaxing and enjoying relief from the cold wetness outside. All of the barstools were occupied, one by a man in a Santa Claus costume who turned and hoisted a glass, proclaiming, "It's a cool Yule on the stool" when he caught Paul's eye. There was no sign of Jane Conroy. Opposite the bar were three booths: a square one in the front corner and two others along the wall. Their benches were black with high backs that separated the tables. The third booth had just been vacated, so Paul claimed it. Santa Claus was admonishing the departing customers to leave a glass of bourbon for him by the fireplace Sunday night. Paul reached into the booth and stood his umbrella on the floor against the dark-wood paneling. Straightening up to take off his coat, he discovered that a waitress had already come over. He recognized her from previous visits but didn't know her name. "Hi," he grinned, pulling out of his left sleeve. "How are you?"

"I'm good." Her round little mouth pushed up into a sort of happy pout. "Would you like a menu?"

"No thanks," folding the coat. "I'll just have a draft. I'm waiting for someone." As she moved away, he worked himself into the booth and sat down facing the doors. The black grandfather clock in the right corner read 12:27. Jane should arrive any minute. He fingered hair back from his forehead and took a pack of cigarettes from his jacket pocket. Then he searched his other pockets: no matches.

The waitress reappeared and carefully placed his brim-full mug of beer on the green-and-white-checked oilcloth. "Thanks." He met her dark eyes. "Would you please bring me some matches?" She could not resist his disarming, blue-eyed smile. She nodded cheerfully and soon returned with two books. He leaned forward and, steadying the mug with his right hand, sipped some of the beer so that it wouldn't spill. Then he lit up and sat back to wait.

He aimed a stream of smoke toward the front door. Jane might be late because of the rain . . . she probably took the eleven-o'clock shuttle. Strange phone call last night. She and John must be having trouble again. Maybe she's going to leave him. There never did seem to be any romance. More like brother and sister. And she could give so much. Cigarette wedged between his first two fingers, he opened and closed, opened and closed a book of matches. "The Tavern O. Henry Made Famous" was printed on the back cover. He often stopped at Pete's for a beer when he was downtown, away from his Columbia neighborhood.

Sipping more beer, he looked around the establishment. One of his favorite bars: a dark, roomy old pub with a restaurant in back. The charm of the place was definitely in its drinking room. A black sign behind the bar asserted in brass-yellow letters, "Oldest Original Bar in New York City Opened 1864." Tinsel-dripping wreaths and winking Xmas lights below it seemed out of place. There was no sawdust on the floor, but there should have been.

The big clock now showed 12:35. The traffic from LaGuardia must be bad. Lunch hour. He stared at the clock. The brass pendulum looked enormous; it moved so slowly and for so short a distance that it seemed likely to stop at any moment. Paul finished his beer and signaled the waitress for another glass. In many of its characteristics, that venerable clock epitomized the tavern: large and rectangular, black and brassy, unexciting but dependable. Although the drinks were not cheap, Paul had seen regulars of vir-

40

tually every description there. And that, of course, made it more interesting. His waitress presented a fresh glass of beer. "Thank you." Skin of bronze, hair of lustrous black, she looked Southeast Asian—perhaps Vietnamese or Thai. He found her warm and appealing. She seemed to blend with the atmosphere.

Again the clock: twelve minutes late. Surely she would've called if she weren't coming. How long since he'd seen her? Jesus, two, two and a half years. Paul lit another cigarette and blew smoke toward the wall of the booth. He noticed a framed clipping on the mirror. Cinnamon-brown and wrinkled with age, *"The World Magazine* Color Gravure Feature Section," datelined "New York, Sunday, December 21, 1930." Today's its anniversary.

He switched places with his coat and edged over for a closer look. The pages contained a reprint of "Gifts of the Magi" by O. Henry. Preceding the short story in italics were explanatory paragraphs relating the discovery of Mr. Porter in Pete's Tavern by two reporters of *The World* in early 1903. The story itself, written by hand in just two hours . . .

Paul saw Jane Conroy's face in the mirror. Before he could rise she had slid into the opposite bench. She leaned forward and they kissed hello. Then she pulled off her scarf and sighed heavily, fluffing her pixie-style auburn hair. My God, she's aged. The last time in Washington she still looked late twenties. Now she looks forty. Her round hazel eyes were rimmed in red. Sunken and tired. "Thanks for coming, Paul."

"Of course." He felt a little sad.

"I know I look awful. I didn't sleep last night."

41

He was uneasy, uncertain. "Don't you want to take off your coat?"

"No." She shuddered. He waited. Then, "John's disappeared." Paul stared at her. He opened his mouth to speak but said nothing. She glanced nervously around at the door, then looked down at the table. "I'm scared." Her voice was weak.

"Has he . . . have things been . . .?"

"No, no," she said. "It's not us. We've been okay. But yesterday he didn't come home. He disappeared!" Her eyes had moistened.

Paul toyed with his cigarette, then reached for her hand. "Tell me what happened."

"May I have a drink?"

"I'm sorry." He turned and craned out of the booth looking for the waitress, but this time couldn't find her. "She'll be right back."

Paul noticed that Santa was watching them. Red-faced St. Nick raised his hand and waved a white-gloved finger in mock scolding, reminding loudly, "Don't forget to hang your stocking with care."

Paul frowned and turned back to Jane. She was dislodging a mangled pack of cigarettes from her purse. Paul gave her one of his and lit it. "Thanks." She exhaled toward the milk-chocolate ceiling. "Yesterday afternoon John went out to buy our Christmas tree, and he didn't come back."

"Was he . . .?"

"When he didn't come home for dinner, I got worried. He wasn't planning to go anywhere else. We were going to trim the tree. So, I started calling around." Her words came nervously in puffs of smoke. "I called every place I could think of. No one had seen him." Jane stared myopically at the end of her cigarette like someone who had just discovered how to inhale. "Finally," her voice broke, "I drove over to the nursery where he always gets our trees. The station wagon was parked there, with Rufus. But no one had seen John." She pulled a handkerchief from her purse.

Paul spotted the waitress and motioned her over. "Jane, what would you like? A martini?"

"No. Something hot. Irish coffee."

"Miss, Irish coffee for the lady, please. Oh, and . . . could you ask them to turn down the jukebox?" The waitress nodded perfunctorily, not pleased.

"I'm really frightened, Paul. All night I kept thinking he'd be coming home . . . or phone."

"Did you call the police?" Paul lit himself another cigarette.

She nodded, wiping her eyes. "Yes. They checked the car last night, but they acted as though it was nothing to worry about. They kept asking me questions about Paul's habits and out marriage . . . as if he'd gone off on a bender or something. It didn't seem to impress them that he'd left the car and dog at the nursery. I kept calling last night and this morning, hoping there'd be some news. They finally listed him as missing, but hadn't found a trace of anything as of noon—I called from LaGuardia."

"What'd they say at the lab? I gather he was off work yesterday."

"They didn't say anything. But I don't trust them there now."

"That sounds worse than usual. Has something happened?"

"God, yes. John quit Tuesday."

"He what? You mean permanently?"

"Yes. He's been thinking about it for months. I thought maybe he'd been in touch with you."

"No. I haven't—"

"He said he was sorry he hadn't resigned when you did, that you were right."

"Wow. That's some switch."

"He got a lot of phone calls Tuesday night and Wednesday morning. Two from Admiral Zimber. John was very nervous and upset. We finally left the phone off the hook."

"What made him decide to quit? Was he still working on the same project?"

"I guess so. I've never known anything about it. John followed the code absolutely." Inhaling deeply, Jane began outlining squares on the tablecloth with her index finger. "Security's been tighter and tighter the last couple of years. The only reason John didn't quit sooner was fear."

"Of what?"

"For his *life.*" She paused as the waitress served her Irish coffee. "He said that one of his assistants left last spring and vanished. He was afraid something might've happened to him. I'm not sure if he believed that, but he's been acting like . . ."

"Go on."

"Well . . . like a man living under a sword." At that instant the jukebox fell silent.

"You think project security grabbed John?!"

She nodded slowly. "John was afraid," she repeated.

They gazed at each other for a few moments. Then

she crushed out her cigarette and took Paul's hand. "That's why I went to a pay phone and wanted to talk to you in person. John thought our phones were probably tapped and that we were all in danger. He said there were rumors that special security assignments were being secretly contracted outside."

"Outside Naval Intelligence?"

Jane sipped her drink, then wiped whipped cream from her mouth. "Outside of everything."

"Sounds like organized crime."

"That's what *he* said."

"Jesus." He squeezed her hand.

"I didn't know where to turn, Paul. I knew I could talk to you and that you might be able to help. I thought because you had been in charge of the lab that maybe you could find something out. Or maybe through Joni's contacts. Do you still see each other?"

"Occasionally." He sat back and exhaled. "I doubt that I can do any good from the inside. Zimber destroyed my reputation there when I resigned. But I'm sure Joni can help. She's getting pretty influential." He leaned forward. "Hell, David Bradford's on Armed Services. He should be able to stir up some action. I'll try to get her now." He started to rise.

"Paul." Jane looked a little brighter and smiled. "Thank you."

He looked into her eyes, then bent across the table and kissed her cheek. "I'll do everything I can. Try to keep cool and not think bad thoughts. Everything may be okay."

Jane glanced at her watch. Her hand was shaking. "I think I'll go right now. I want to get back as soon as possible, and there's still time to catch the two-o'clock flight." She took another gulp of coffee, then sidled to her left and stood up.

"Look, Jane, I'll call you just as soon as I have anything to report." Paul's cigarette dangled from his mouth, dribbling ashes as he extricated himself from the booth.

"Let me call you instead."

"Well . . . all right."

"Will you be home later this afternoon?"

"Yes. I've got to turn in some grades, but I should be back by four."

"What about tonight?"

"I'll be there. I was going out of town, but that can wait." He took her hand. "I'll come down to Washington myself if we don't get anywhere soon. I can blow Zimber's little empire right out of the water if I have to." Jane was beginning to cry again. The room noise had become noticeably louder. "I'll get you a cab. It's raining pretty hard."

"No, don't bother." She sniffed. "You're not responsible for the weather. I've got my umbrella, and I'm sure I can find a taxi on Park. Your phone calls are more important."

As they walked toward the door, the swaying Santa Claus at the bar was shouting something about bourbon. Over the din of lunch-hour conversation arose a booming "Ho! Ho! . . . Ho!" punctuated by a belch between the last two ho's.

"You sure about the cab?"

"I'm sure." She retied her orange scarf, then gently pressed her fingertips against Paul's lips. "Don't worry, I'm okay." He nodded and they kissed goodbye. She pushed out through the doors, looking

46

like a little girl bundled up against the storm. Paul could see snow mixing with the rain as he watched Jane cross the street. It was unusually dark for midday—like the dimness of dusk. Or of solar eclipse.

5

WASHINGTON NATIONAL AIRPORT:
3:00 PM, THURSDAY, DECEMBER 21

TEMPERATURE: 31°F

BAROMETER: 29.69″ (FALLING)

WIND: ENE 15–20 MPH

PRECIPITATION: MODERATE SNOW (3″)

FORECAST: SNOW ENDING BY EVENING,
CLEARING AND COLD TONIGHT

Arnold Berger was speeding southbound on the Capital Beltway a few miles northwest of the District of Columbia. He slowly shook his head in disgust for having had to make an unanticipated and, he was

48

convinced, totally unnecessary trip to the National Oceanic and Atmospheric Administration (NOAA) in Rockville. There was already enough to do with Conroy gone. Son of a bitch—chickening out at the last minute. A little more warning would've helped. Oh well, good riddance. He was a worrier . . . and a liability.

Snow was falling heavily and beginning to accumulate on the pavement. All lanes were now white. The windshield wipers worked monotonously against the melting flakes: schlump-flump, schlump-flump. Soon the freeway began its gradual descent into the valley of the Potomac River. A gust of wind spiraled snow across the road like a gigantic spectral tumbleweed. The swirling cloud engulfed a sign on the right shoulder, almost obscuring its message: SNOW ROUTE.

As he approached the Cabin John Bridge, a large complex of white buildings materialized on the right. It was hard to make out in the storm—it looked sort of like an elaborate snow fort. NAVAL SHIP RESEARCH AND DEVELOPMENT CENTER was painted on the front. Berger turned right into the entrance road and drove a long distance to the rear of the buildings, where he parked at the side of a snow-covered lot near the river. The Potomac lay pale algid gray under the slanting snow. Low and still, it languished its icy way from the closing recesses of an albescent haze. Not far upstream huddled a cluster of snow-coated rocks masquerading as coconut cupcakes.

Berger grabbed his briefcase, locked the car, and trotted to the rear of the closest building. He unlocked the outside door and entered. The security guard behind a thick glass window greeted him and opened the inner door by remote control as a miniature television camera looked on. After depositing his coat in his office, Berger walked to an elevator and punched the coded sequence of numbers that would take him to the second level in the basement. Smoothly and silently downward.

He adjusted his black-framed glasses and looked at his watch as he strode rapidly along the familiar underground corridor. His gait was stiff and mechanical. Berger's shining black hair was neatly parted and held in place by spray. Dark eyes close-set and intense, his sallow masklike face was imprinted with earnestness, looking as though it would be physically difficult for it to relax into a smile. Bright young Arnold Berger took himself very seriously. As the new project director, he had important responsibilities for someone only thirty years old.

Upon reaching a blue door marked NO ADMITTANCE, he made an obscene gesture to a television camera, and the door opened. Inside, another security guard returned his salute and remotely ushered him through a second door. Then Berger typed numbers and letters on a wall keyboard and passed through a sliding panel to enter a large, brightly illuminated room.

Along its left side was a row of eight computer consoles. Seated before all but two were unsmiling operators wearing headsets. Behind them on the left-hand wall stretched a map of the earth; sweeping across it were wavelike lines; marking the paths of artificial satellites whose orbits transected the equator. A relief map on the back wall of the room represented part of the northern hemisphere, including North America, the North Atlantic, North Africa, and most of Eurasia. Little light bulbs of red and green decorated the continents. About half were lit. Small numbered disks were scattered across the Atlantic. To the right, three men were leaning over an immense drafting table covered by overlapping charts. On the wall beyond, a projection screen ten feet wide displayed a live black-and-white satellite image of part of the earth. It seemed to consist largely of clouds. A battery of digital clocks above the screen showed the time in adjacent zones. The one labeled EST read 15:14.

A tall Black man wearing an open plaid shirt immediately approached Berger. "Get 'em?" he asked.

"Yes. In here." Berger opened his briefcase.

"Carl," the other called to a short man with thick glasses who was standing next to one of the teletype units, "we've got the new NOAA keys." Carl hurried over and Berger handed him a deck of computer cards and a sheaf of folded printout paper.

"Berger's delivery service," announced Berger. Carl smiled, cautiously peering over the tops of his glasses. Then he walked quickly away. Berger sighed and turned to his companion. "You know, George, it's unbelievable that we're in this kind of situation and have almost zero clout. We're so secret, we're unknown quantities. *Nobody* trusts us." They moved over to the large table. "It's ridiculous that I should have to waste time going up there to pound the table just because they didn't bother to tell us they were changing their codes." He put his hands on his hips and looked up at the projection screen. "Well, shit. What's the latest?"

"More problems." George Williams' voice told Berger that the problems were serious. "The good ship *Narwhal* reports negative response since fifteen hundred hours."

The two men looked at each other silently for a moment. Then Berger asked softly, "Nothing?"

George nodded slowly. "Absolute zero."

Berger gazed at the floor, taking off his glasses and rubbing his right eye. "Got 'em on direct voice now?"

"Oh, yes." The two started for a door just to the left of the cloudy screen.

Admiral Curtis Zimber looked at his watch: 4:05. After a tense meeting in the White House, he was looking forward to his cocktail party in Rockville. Northbound on 16th Street, his chauffeur was driving conservatively because of the traffic and the snow. In spite of the bad weather and early rush hour, they should be able to get home well before five. The Admiral was confident that he had been effective, even impressive, that afternoon in fielding questions about his proposed drone-submarine project. He could expound upon that little triumph for hours. And at the same time he could secretly celebrate his other achievement of the day.

Admiral Zimber's limousine was motoring smoothly through the settling snow. The air was almost calm; the snow seemed to absorb and soften all sounds. From inside the moving car, however, the flakes appeared to be flying straight back into the windshield as if driven by a gale. Most of them swept over the top or brushed past the sides of the vehicle, but some plastered themselves against it. Snow had already covered the rows of sandy slush along the street, turning them whitish.

As they passed Walter Reed Army Medical Center on the right, the Admiral snorted and bent forward to open his large leather briefcase. From a medium-sized jiffy bag he withdrew a pint flask and poured amber liquid into a coffee mug. He noticed that the driver was watching him in the rear-view mirror. "Little coffee here, Crawford. Got to fortify against this weather." He toasted and took a sip.

"Yes, sir. Jim Beam's finest coffee," clucked Crawford.

Admiral Zimber was smiling as he gazed out the window. On display to their left was part of the eastern edge of Rock Creek Park. Five inches of fresh snow had transformed its naked stand of sticks into a picturesque holiday snowscape. Stark trees had been softly decorated by a generous trimming of white, each crisp twig neatly hidden beneath its fluffy covering. The limber branches of occasional ever-greens swept downward under pillowed drapery, and lowly bushes bowed to the smooth white earth in re-spectful submission. The fresh purity of this winter beauty demeaned the seasonal profusion of electrical jewelry that bespangled buildings across the street. "The snow's beautiful, eh, Crawford?" The Admiral appeared to be toasting the view through his window.

"Yes, sir. But I could appreciate it more if I didn't have to drive in it." The passing scenes seemed al-most illusory through the dancing filter of descending snowflakes. Seen through the windshield, the onrush-ing flakes fashioned a special perspective. They di-verged as they drew near the vehicle, evoking the sensation of hurtling into a funnel. "Keeps on much longer, it'll really tie up this town," Crawford added.

"The storm is due to end this evening," the Admi-ral assured him and took another sip.

"I don't know. You just never can tell about the weather. Nobody predicted this much snow for today in the first place." Crawford stuck a toothpick into his mouth.

"Well, we'll see." Zimber added some fluid to his mug and sat back. " 'Hard winters are good for body and soul,' my father used to say. You know I grew up in northern Wisconsin?"

"Yes, sir. You've told me. Ever do any snowmobilin'?"

"No. Hell no. I hate those goddam things." Another sip. "They weren't around then. Couldn't've afforded to fool with 'em even if they had been. No, my favorite winter sport was icefishing. I used to go with my father. Great fun."

"Wasn't your father raised in China?" Crawford inquired.

"Yes, partly. My grandfather was a missionary there. But he died as a young man, so Grandmother brought the family back to the States. Father was killed fighting for the Chinese in 1938—my first year at Annapolis."

Soon after turning onto north Georgia Avenue, they approached the Capital Beltway. "Northern Virginia": snow-white words on Interstate green. Crawford took the second right, looping back to merge westbound with INTERSTATE MARYLAND 495. The middle lane had a gap, so he pushed down the directional lever and eased over into it. Traffic was heavy for 4:30 on a Thursday.

"That Mormon temple is really impressive. Looks a little spooky through the snow." The driver was leaning forward and squinting through the windshield. Slowly solidifying over the vaporous horizon were the spires of an alabaster castle soaring to the clouds. Through its niveous veil, the ghostly edifice seemed to be hovering above the whitened hillsides, pinnacles quivering as if in mirage. As they drove closer, the image sharpened and its airy feeling of fantasy hardened into cool slab surfaces and straight vertical lines. Rectilinear white towers necked down in steps to square pedestals supporting golden minarets: metallic needles piercing the milky sky. Atop the closest and tallest spire, a gilded figure facing the east appeared to be sounding a horn, perhaps of rejoicing or warning. Then an unfelt breath of wind rippled sheer curtains of falling snow over the face of the shrine, resurrecting its aura of unreality. Smooth, cold-white, and crystalline. A glacial cathedral sculptured from an iceberg.

Crawford watched the temple draw behind the slopes above them and vanish into whiteness. "Up in the snow and clouds that way, it looks like a monument to the Ice Age or something. Have you been up there, Admiral?"

"Yeah. Just a flashy showpiece." Curtis Zimber pulled off his cap and scratched his frizzy gray hair, then took another sip from his mug. "Must've cost a fortune," he muttered. "Goddam waste of money."

It seemed to be getting darker and more difficult to see, so Crawford pulled on the headlights as they were crossing over Connecticut Avenue. Ahead on the left, a snow-covered car was parked on the shoulder of the eastbound lanes. It seemed to be turned at an awkward angle. Looking straight across the median as they passed, Admiral Zimber could see that the dark sedan was perpendicular to the highway, its back wheels resting in a snowy depression. "People around here just don't have enough experience driving in winter weather," he commented.

"Well, they're going to get some," said Crawford. "It's really snowing hard."

"It's thicker, all right. Wind's picking up again too. That I don't like." Outside, a line of massed evergreens brandished in the breeze like a phalanx of rebellious Christmas trees. The flashing amber beacon of a snowplow came into view just ahead, so Crawford moved into the left-hand lane to go around it. There were several inches of snow on the unplowed side, and the differences in sound and feel were immediately noticeable: more muffled, more resistant. As they passed by, the bulky truck was cascading quantities of snow over a sign which cautioned EMERGENCY STOPPING ONLY. The snow from the sky was angling across the highway right-to-left on a persistent north-northeast breeze.

The red light on the Admiral's radiophone lit. "Phone call. May I have privacy, Crawford?"

"Yes, sir," and the glass moved up to separate the driver from the rear of the limousine. It was 4:39.

"Zimber here." The Admiral was clutching his mug. "Who?" There was a pause, then, "All right. Yes. Yes. What?" Liquid sloshed over the lip of his cup. "Don't say any more. Don't say any more! I'll call you from a booth." Another pause. "Yes, yes. I have the number, and for God's sake, don't say it!" Zimber hung up. His fleshy face was perspiring as he leaned forward and rapped sharply on the glass partition. It lowered. "Crawford, get me to a phone booth immediately."

"Yes, sir. Is your radiophone not workin'?"

"No questions. Move." They took Rockville Pike back to Bethesda.

In ten minutes the stout Admiral slammed into a

56

phone booth next to a service station. "This is Zimber 774-401. Give me the report." He listened. Then, "None at all?" And, "*No* other explanation?" Finally, "All right, get Popowski to my office immediately. I'll meet him. We'll take it from there." His chest heaved a deep breath; his shirt collar was stained with sweat. "Christ, I don't know. Give me forty-five minutes." He clanged down the receiver and pushed out of the booth. Two boys nearby were having a snowball fight.

"You're dead."

"The heck I am."

"Yes you are."

"No I'm not."

"You are too."

"I am *not*. You missed me a mile."

"Listen, frog-brain, that snowball had a rock in it."

"So what?"

"That means it was a magnum grenade an' you're dead."

They must have been about nine or ten.

"No I'm not."

"Yes you *are!*"

Curtis Zimber charged into his limousine. "Pentagon." Snow lay thickly in the street, plowed into loose furrows by churning wheels.

6

~~~~~~

LOGAN INTERNATIONAL AIRPORT:
   7:00 PM, THURSDAY, DECEMBER 21

TEMPERATURE: 28°F

BAROMETER: 29.86″ (FALLING)

WIND: SE 14–24 MPH

PRECIPITATION: HEAVY SNOW (6″)

FORECAST: SNOW ENDING TONIGHT,
   CLEARING AND COLDER TOMORROW

Klumph! The door of the Boeing 727 had finally been shut; a stewardess turned the handle into locking position. From his left-hand window seat in the first-class cabin, Harvey Meyer watched the enclosed ramp back slowly away from the nose of the jet. Light from overhanging floodlamps formed bright cones illuminating swarms of snowflakes sweeping to the ground. Soft ruts just made by a retreating baggage shuttle seemed to be about six inches deep.

Engine noise was barely audible as the big plane rolled backward and turned away from the gate. Harvey glanced at the cockpit door, then removed his silver-framed glasses and massaged the bridge of his nose and corners of his eyes with a thumb and index finger. He supposed that he should be satisfied to be leaving at all in such disagreeable weather.

The intercom came alive with a click and brief shuffle of static. "This is your captain speaking. Welcome aboard Flight 269 for Chicago. We're sorry about the delay, just as you are, but the snowstorm has everything in and out of Boston running behind schedule this evening. Right now we're twenty-third in line for takeoff and . . ."

"Je-zus Christ!" from the large, restless man on Meyer's right.

". . . been waiting for snow-removal equipment to finish clearing the one runway that's operating. So, it'll be at least thirty minutes until we get away. I'm going to turn off the no-smoking sign, and the cabin attendants will serve you complimentary beverages while there's time before departure." Chime!—off went the sign.

"Thirty minutes, my ass," again from the right. "I'll believe that when it happens. It's their policy to underestimate delays just to keep down the gripin'."

Meyer leaned over and pulled his attaché case from under the forward seat. He carefully removed a copy of *The Wall Street Journal* and, straightening up, glanced sideways over the rims of his glasses. The large man was watching. He thrust a big hand toward Harvey, a broad but plastic smile creasing his ruddy face beneath a prominent nose and piercing gray-blue eyes. "Matthew Rodek," he announced with obvious pleasure.

"I'm happy to meet you. My name is Harvey Meyer." Harvey's hand disappeared in the other's grip but was not quite crushed.

Leaning back in his seat, Rodek lamented, "I shoulda known when I made a nine-o'clock dinner reservation that this storm'd get worse an' screw things up. You gettin' off in Chicago?"

"No, continuing on to Denver." Harvey palmed wavy gray hair on the back of his head into place, then flattened out the front page of his paper.

"That's a great area." Rodek crossed his legs, bumping the back of the seat in front of him. "Are you a skier?"

"No, I'm not," Meyer responded, still looking at his newspaper.

"Excuse me, sir. Would you care for a cocktail before takeoff?" The tall dark stewardess was wearing wet-looking red lipstick.

"Hi, doll. Bourbon on the rocks. I suppose you're gonna give us those plastic glasses."

"While we're on the ground." She smiled flatly. Then, looking over at Harvey, "And you, sir?"

"Scotch and water, please."

"Thank you." And she turned to passengers across the aisle. The jet was edging forward and about to enter the main line of waiting planes. Landing lights penetrated the darkness in beams of countless white flakes.

"Boy, she's a big one, huh?" Rodek was watching the stewardess; his lips drew back into a thin grin of yellow teeth. Whitening hair was clumped on both sides of his balding head above medium-length sideburns. His neighbor was reading and offered no comment. Rodek sat upright. "What's your line out there in Colorado?"

"I'm in the sugar business." With arched eyebrows, Meyer methodically turned the page.

"Farming?"

"Would you care for a magazine, sir?" This stewardess was shorter and blond.

"Uh, yeah, honey. *Sports Illustrated?*"

"I'm sorry, sir, I just gave away the last copy. Let's see . . . how about *Outdoor Life?*"

"Well, okay." He turned to the contents page.

She looked at Harvey. "Thank you, no."

"That's one reason I'd like to live out in your country," Rodek explained. "There's a lotta damn good huntin'." He loosened his red-and-white tie. Glancing up, "You say you run a sugar farm?"

"My firm owns and operates a number of sugar-beet properties," Harvey explained indifferently.

"I'm retired myself," Rodek volunteered.

"You seem rather young to be retired," without looking up.

"Thirty years in the Navy was long enough," came the emphatic reply. "And most of it under water."

"Submarines?"

"That's right. In fact, I'm just on my way back from New London. Had a special assignment there."

"I don't think I'd care for submarines," Harvey confessed, turning toward his companion. "I'm afraid I'd get claustrophobia."

"You get over it," Rodek assured him. "And the pay is good—especially if you're single. I've been in all kinds of subs: from the big nukes to a two-man deep submersible. Remember that Russian sub the CIA brought up a few years back?"

"Yes. That was a fascinating disclosure."

"Yeah, well, I piloted the vessel that did it—old Nessie. Talk about scary. Christ, the pressure down there—two thousand fathoms—is enough to squeeze ya inta nothin'.''

Rodek noticed movement in the aisle. "Ah, here comes the booze. 'Bout time." The plane crept forward another place or two in line. He glanced back at Harvey Meyer. "Sugar beets are mostly in southeastern Colorado, aren't they?"

"That's correct."

"Yeah. I hear it's hot as hell down there in the summer." And the drinks arrived.

After pulling out his table and emptying both little bottles into his glass, Rodek proposed a toast. "Well, Meyers, here's hoping we get off tonight." He raised his glass conspicuously and, tilting his head slightly downward, peered out from under raised eyebrows and wrinkled forehead in order to emphasize that his toast was not entirely in jest. Meyer nodded in silent acknowledgment.

"I suppose you have to irrigate?" Rodek persisted.

"Oh yes, that's one of our principal expenses." Harvey took a first sip of his drink.

"Ever try cloud seedin'?" And Matthew swallowed some of his.

"Yes, as a matter of fact." Meyer wiped his mouth with a handkerchief and looked at Rodek. "My partners talked me into a contract with so-called rain-makers the summer before last."

"How'd it work?"

"It didn't." Harvey looked back at his *Journal*.

"We did a lot of that weather modification in Southeast Asia—and not just in Nam, either. The CIA's been pushin' it for a long time." Matthew took a gulp. "Russians and Chinese are into it too."

"Oh?" Eyebrows up. "I didn't realize that."

"There's a lot goes on most people don't know about," Rodek said softly as though revealing some profound secret. A fuel truck passed by, headlights probing the snow-filled air. "Goddam, it's really comin' down." Rodek rose and leaned over his companion for a better view out the window. In the process he spilled a few drops of bourbon into the lap of Meyer's absorbent tweed suitpants. "Oh, sorry." And then, "Huh! There goes another one . . . they're still takin' off. Hey, take a gander at that friggin' tower." He pointed. "You can hardly see it."

At length he sat down again, and Meyer eased forward to look out. The Logan Airport tower was blurred and uncommonly eerie through the snow, a giant biped challenging the storm. Their jet moved again.

Sipping his Scotch and water, Harvey returned to the paper. His complexion was smooth and sallow, his eyes almost black. He had nearly completed the first paragraph of an article discussing fertilizer sales to China when his neighbor proclaimed accusingly, "That's the worst-designed airport tower I've ever seen!"

Meyer eyed him with mild skepticism. "Is that so?"

Rodek drained his remaining bourbon and jabbed

the call button with a middle finger. Chime! "Hell yes. I hear it's so damn tall that every time the ceiling comes down they can't even see the runways. Now take tonight—Oh, another bourbon on the rocks, doll. You want another, Meyers?"

"No, thank you."

"I'm surprised the top of that tower isn't in the clouds already." The plane rolled forward once more. Rodek looked at his watch. "Christ, almost an hour late! We'll be lucky to get to O'Hare by nine. You might know we'd get an unexpected storm. This wasnt predicted, you know," he announced.

"Yes, I don't recall snow having been in the forecast this morning." Harvey put down his *Journal*, temporarily giving up the struggle to read.

"Here you are, sir." Rodek accepted the new drink with a nod and slight compression of his lips, then arranged the bottles and glass on his table.

He continued as he poured. "I was watchin' the news tonight in the Admirals Club. This storm is spread all to hell 'n' gone along the East Coast." Turning to Meyer, "It's snowin' in D.C., rain an' snow in the Big Apple."

Meyer noticed that when his loquacious acquaintance was making a point, his face would tighten as though strained by concentration. With head cocked to one side, eyebrows pulled into vertical furrows, and eyes rounded to acute intensity, he reminded him of a vigilant hound waiting for the repetition of an ill-defined sound. "Rain and snow where?"

"New York." Rodek flipped his hand toward the window. "There's no excuse for this long holdup. They don't know what the hell they're doin' here.

Can't handle surprise storms—which is most of 'em."
He took another swallow. "If this storm lasts . . ."

Static. "Well, folks, we're third in line for takeoff
now, so I'm going to have to turn the no-smoking
sign back on. Please check to make sure that your
seatbelts are securely fastened." Chime!

"Huh! I guess we'll finally get outa here. I shoulda
canceled my dinner date before I got on the plane.
Now I'll hafta phone from O'Hare."

"May I take your glasses, gentlemen?"
Rodek gulped down the rest of his bourbon and
quickly wrestled out of his black-and-white-plaid
suitcoat. "Can you hang this?" The tall stewardess
was holding a plastic trash bag. She dropped their
empty glasses into it.

"I'll be glad to as soon as we reach cruising alti-
tude. Please return your seatback to the upright
position and fasten your seatbelt." He promptly
complied, folding the coat in his lap and rearranging
his large frame with exaggerated motions. Then he
sat back and closed his eyes. At this hopeful sign,
Harvey Meyer reopened *The Wall Street Journal.*

The intercom: "Flight attendants please prepare
for takeoff."

Meyer could see billowing swirls of snow stirred up
by the jet blast of an aircraft in front of them as it
vanished into grayness. At last it was their turn. The
trio of engines on the tail began accelerating even
before they had completed their swing onto the runway. Vibrations increased and increased, then ceased
as the plane lifted into the night. It tilted its nose upward at what seemed to be an unusually steep angle.

Chime! Immediately the snap of a cigarette lighter.
Rodek was beginning to snore. Harvey became

conscious of a change at his window, so he shielded his eyes from the cabin lights and peered through the glass.

The shining jet had emerged from the pale sea below and seemed suspended in stillness under a whole sky of stars. The calm purity of the view was captivating. Harvey watched wispy plumes curling up from the main cloud layer; they moved steadily backward toward the east. The smooth whiteness underneath stretched to the horizon wherever he could see, concealing all beneath it. It might have been a great expanse of wind-skimmed snow—as in photographs of the surface of the Antarctic ice cap. Or a dimpled blanket of cotton just laid for a decorative winter scene under a holiday tree. Harvey leaned back in his seat; he was thinking of presents in his suitcase.

Static. "This is Captain Holmes. We want to apologize again for the long wait in Boston. However, we should be able to gain a few minutes between here and Chicago so that we'll be at the gate no more than one hour behind our scheduled arrival time. The weather at O'Hare is clear with a temperature of 21 degrees. If it's any consolation, we were fortunate to get airborne when we did. Because of drifting snow and poor visibility, Logan International Airport has just been closed."

7

~~~~~~

MANHATTAN, ROCKEFELLER CENTER:
   8:00 PM, THURSDAY, DECEMBER 21

TEMPERATURE: 29°F

BAROMETER: 29.60″ (FALLING)

WIND: ESE 18–30 MPH

PRECIPITATION: HEAVY SNOW (6″)

FORECAST: SNOW ENDING BY MORNING,
   CLEARING AND COLDER

"I've been trying to reach you since lunch, Joni, but
no one knew where you were." Paul glanced at the
clock in his kitchen. It was 8:15.

"I'm sorry. I wish I could've known. I took the afternoon off and went shopping. Then I got stuck in traffic on the way home. This snow is tying everything up."

"I'm glad I got you at all. It's a bad time to find people. I was afraid you'd gone out of town."

"No. Look, Paul, I'll get right on this Conroy matter. First I'll call the police myself to find out what's happening. Then I'll phone David Bradford. Since it's a possible kidnapping, I'm sure he can get the feds on it. Are you sure Jane Conroy wouldn't like me to call her?"

"That's the way it sounded. She's afraid to use her phone. But she said she'd call me. When she does, I'll ask her to get in touch with you."

"That would help. I'm in for the night now. Well, I'd better get started."

"Okay. Uh . . . how have you been?"

"Fine. Busy. And you? You sound well."

"Oh, I'm in good shape. I was planning to drive to Vermont this afternoon to go skiing, but I postponed that because of Conroy. The storm probably would've held us up anyway."

"I'll call if there's any news, Paul. But I doubt that we'll learn anything before morning."

"All right. It's good to hear your voice. Makes me miss you."

"Yes, it would be good to see you. Good night."

"Good night."

"Please stay in your seats until the aircraft has come to a complete stop at the gate," urged one of the flight attendants as the jet from Boston eased into position at O'Hare.

Matthew Rodek tightened his necktie and sat back

down. He turned to his companion. "You gonna stretch your legs, Meyers?"

"No, I think I'll stay on board."

"Buy you a drink. I'm late for dinner anyway."

"Thank you, no. It was nice to meet you."

"Same here. Say, ya know—"

The loudspeaker came on again. "Passenger Matthew Rodek, please identify yourself to one of the flight attendants. Passenger Matthew Rodek . . ."

Rodek jabbed the call button. The tall, dark stewardess promptly appeared. "Are you Mr. Rodek?"

"That's me, doll." His brow rippled. "What's up?"

"We have a message for you. An agent is waiting at the door. Will you come with me, please?"

"Sure." He hesitated, then, "Yeah. Okay." Rodek grabbed his briefcase. "See ya, Meyers." He followed the young lady forward and pulled his topcoat and apparel bag from the closet. A uniformed airline agent was waiting for him when the 727's door opened.

"Commander Rodek?"

"That's right."

"We have a message for you. Please follow me." They walked rapidly down the jetway into the lounge, where the agent beckoned him to one side. "A Mr. Walter Popowski of the Department of the Navy in Washington has requested that you telephone him immediately at his office. He said that you had the number."

"Yeah, I've got it." Rodek was frowning. "Is that all?"

"Mr. Popowski said to tell you that it was extremely important."

Rodek glanced at a nearby pay phone. "Okay,

thanks. He hurried over to it. In a moment Walter Popowski was on the line.

"That's right, Rodek. A helicopter is enroute to O'Hare now. It will take you to Great Lakes, where a Navy jet will be waiting to fly you back to New London. Call the airport manager's office for instructions on meeting the chopper. You will be briefed on the situation after your arrival in Connecticut. That's all I can tell you now. Any questions?"

"I guess not." Matthew was reloosening his tie. "I guess I'd better make a couple of quick calls."

"The big story tonight, of course, is the weather." The natty newsman looked up. "Travel throughout much of the Northeast has been brought to a virtual standstill by what has now become one of the worst snowstorms in recent years." Paul Garfield was watching the 11:00 news from his bed. He leaned forward and pulled another pillow behind his back to prop himself more comfortably against the headboard. Shirtless and barefoot, he was wearing an old pair of bluejeans cut off just above the knee. He still retained a trace of fading summer suntan.

"Earlier tonight the National Weather Service issued winter storm warnings for parts of eleven states from Virginia to Maine." A map of the northeastern United States appeared on the television screen, showing a strip along the coast shaded in white. A bold "L" was positioned offshore on the Atlantic due east of Chesapeake Bay.

"Heavy snow has been falling throughout this area," an anonymous pointer was pointing, "since early this afternoon, and unusually heavy snow has continued to accumulate tonight all the way from the

70

nation's capital up to Boston. The effects of the snow-fall are now being magnified by drifting due to increasing winds, which range from fifteen to thirty-five miles per hour with gusts up to fifty miles per hour in some coastal areas. Small-craft warnings . . ."

The phone rang. Maybe it's Jane. Paul lifted the receiver at the end of its second ring. "Hello," he said, trying to sound cheerful.

"Paul Garfield?" asked a baritone voice.

"Speaking." Paul didn't recognize it.

"This is David Bradford."

"Hello." He was genuinely surprised. "How *are* you, David?"

"I'm well, thanks. Yourself?"

"Good. It's been a long time."

"It surely has. I often think of you. In fact, Joni had an appointment with me yesterday morning and I asked about you. I gather you're happy at Columbia."

"Yes, pretty much. It's good to be back in astrophysics." Poquito flew over from the rubber tree and landed on the green quilt at the foot of the bed. Their colors nearly matched.

"I suppose it's quite a change from your work at ONR"—Office of Naval Research.

"That's for sure. Campus politics is more my speed. I've been reading a lot about you lately, and, in spite of my former employment, I want to say that I support your position on defense waste."

"Thank—"

"And your efforts to do something about it. That's what's been needed. It takes political courage to follow through." Paul took a sip from a can of beer. He would wait for the Senator to change the subject.

71

"Thank you, Paul, I don't often hear that. We should keep in closer touch—I need your kind of encouragement. Do you come to Washington much?"

"No." Paul swallowed. "Not since I left the lab. But I would enjoy seeing you again."

"Please call me any time. You'll get right through."

"Thanks, David. I will."

"Paul." The Senator's voice tightened. "I received a call from Joni a few minutes ago—Carla and I had gone to a friend's for dinner and had just come home. By the way, the snow is so deep we had to leave our car and walk back. Fortunately, it was only two blocks. At any rate, Joni explained to me the unfortunate situation involving John Conroy. Of course I agreed to look into it. Because of the time lapse since she talked to you, I felt that I should phone you directly to express my concern and willingness to help."

"I appreciate that very much, David." Paul wriggled into a more upright position. The parakeet was pulling a down feather out of the quilt.

"Joni said that Mrs. Conroy was afraid to use her telephone. Nonetheless, I tried to call her. But there was no answer."

"She may have gone out to use another phone."

"It's a bad night to do that."

"Here too."

"I did speak to the Montgomery County Sheriff's Office. As yet they have nothing to report regarding Conroy's disappearance. And, of course, they have their hands full tonight with this heavy snowstorm." Senator Bradford cleared his throat. "The FBI, however, assured me that they would begin an immediate investigation predicated on the assumption of kidnapping. An associate director personally promised to have a report telephoned to me at nine A.M."

"That's excellent, David. I know it will be a comfort to Jane. I'll tell her if she calls. She seems to think that John's disappearance is related to his resignation from ONR."

"He was still working with your old group, wasn't he?"

"Yes." Paul swallowed more beer and put the can on the floor.

"Who oversees that work?"

"It's a highly secret, bastard sort of group. Admiral Curtis Zimber controls the funding."

There was a lengthy pause. "We shouldn't talk about this on the telephone." David Bradford's voice had become more animated. "When convenient, could you come down to Washington at my expense to discuss the situation further?"

Paul hesitated for a moment. Then, "Yes. But gladly at my own expense." He wanted it to be his own idea.

"Could you come next week—after Christmas?" came the quick reply.

"All right . . . that should be okay." Paul cradled the receiver between his neck and shoulder and lit a cigarette.

"Good. Think about a particular day. I can work you in anytime. I'll call again in the morning after I hear from the FBI. Will you be in?"

"I'll be here. Snowed in, the way it looks."

"Let's hope not. Well, it's been good talking to you, Paul. I'll let you go. Mrs. Conroy may be trying to call you."

"David?" Paul's tone was more personal.

"Yes, Paul?"

"How has Joni been doing? We don't talk much these days."

"She seems to be doing beautifully. I hear a lot of good things. She has a great deal going for her."

"I know."

"Yes, you surely do. We'll never disagree on Joni."

"No, I guess not. Uh, is she still . . . unattached?"

"As far as I know, Paul."

"Well," Paul hesitated, "thanks again for calling, Senator."

"You're most welcome. Talk to you tomorrow."

They hung up simultaneously. Paul smoked his cigarette, staring blankly at the television screen. Details of the news were now being presented following a commercial.

". . . and at eleven o'clock, snow depths in the five boroughs ranged from nine to thirteen inches. A gusty wind out of the east is piling snow into drifts several feet deep, as much as five feet deep on Long Island. Although the Department of Sanitation has put some three thousand men and fifteen hundred vehicles to work on the city's six thousand miles of streets, the rapidly drifting snow and numerous stalled and abandoned vehicles are making it almost impossible to keep the traffic lanes open. Needless to say—"

At that moment a man in shirtsleeves approached the news desk and handed the reporter a sheet of paper. After nodding, the latter began reading from it. "The mayor has just declared a snow emergency in the City of New York. The principal purpose of this action is to facilitate the job of clearing the city's streets. Only cars with chains or snow tires will be allowed on designated snow streets until the emergency is lifted. Alternate-side-of-the-street parking regulations are suspended to . . ."

"Oh, Jesus," Paul complained. How could he possibly move his car?

"Snow emergencies have also been declared on Long Island, in Westchester and Rockland counties, and in northern New Jersey. Jersey City has banned all but essential vehicles from most of its roads." The newscaster looked up at the camera. "The fact that these emergency declarations seem to have been issued somewhat after the fact is simply an indication of just how fast this storm situation has developed." Paul exhaled.

The reporter returned to his script. "Travel should not be attempted tonight except in the case of a critical emergency—and then only with the assistance of a specially equipped vehicle. Many motorists have been stranded, particularly in some of the outlying areas. At news time, nineteen fatalities had already been attributed directly or indirectly to the effects of this storm, and the National Safety Council late this evening expressed fears that the death toll may rise considerably higher by morning among motorists whose cars have stalled.

"The principal dangers are exposure and carbon monoxide poisoning. The advice of the National Safety Council is twofold: First, do not abandon your vehicle unless other shelter is immediately available, and second, bundle up to keep warm as well as you can inside your vehicle with one window open a fraction of an inch for fresh air. Under *no* circumstances leave your motor running for use of the heater." He

75

glanced up. "Leaky exhaust systems are all too common," and he looked back down. "Deadly carbon-monoxide gas may find its way into your vehicle. These toxic fumes are odorless and colorless. You may intend to run the motor for just a few minutes, but if you should fall asleep, you might never wake up. Don't risk it." Paul was scratching the blondish hair on his chest. This motion attracted Poquito's attention; the bird flew up to perch on the headboard behind Paul's shoulder. "Householders who see stranded motorists are urged by the National Safety Council to offer them shelter."

The reporter turned over a page. "All three metropolitan airports were effectively closed by ten o'clock tonight as airlines canceled remaining flights due to low visibility and drifting snow on the runways. The Port Authority of New York and New Jersey expects regular service to be resumed in the morning as soon as runways can be cleared."

"Hmmmh," Paul grunted. "Schedules'll be screwed up for two days." He felt on the floor for his half-empty can of beer.

". . . Long Island Railroad has announced that its more than one hundred thousand commuter passengers will have to find other means of transportation into the city tomorrow morning because it does not expect to complete snow-clearing operations in time for rush hour. It suspended all its service about an hour ago. In addition, announcements of all sorts of closings and cancellations for tonight and tomorrow have been pouring in since late this afternoon, so we suggest that you recheck your own situation before leaving home in the morning. And now," the newscaster's eyebrows rose, "let's see just how bad it is out there tonight."

The scene changed. "Here our portable camera is in Central Park." The lower half of the screen was entirely white except for a few dark lines and patches, probably trees and rocks. And these wobbled erratically as if the camera were unsteady. The upper half of the screen was a blurry rippling of what appeared to be waves of snow blowing through the light of a street lamp. "As you can see, Old Man Winter ignored the forecasts and followed the calendar, arriving right on schedule. If you didn't know it already, today is officially the first day of winter."

"And the last day of Chanukah," prompted a voice in the background.

Back to the studio. "That's right, ladies and gentlemen. Dr. Jake just reminded me that today is also the last of the eight holy days of Chanukah on the Judaic calendar. Happy Chanukah." The newscaster smiled insipidly, then again referred to his script. "Although conditions are bad enough here, New York has actually fared better than some of the other affected areas. For example, by eleven P.M. snowfall in the nation's capital measured fourteen inches. The storm center that's causing all the trouble is a big one and has been stalled over the Atlantic east of Washington, D.C., since this morning." Paul sat up straighter and finished his beer. The parakeet was marching up and down the headboard. "It *is* expected to move farther offshore and bring an end to the snow within the next few hours. The National Weather Service now predicts no more than one to two additional inches of snow." He looked to his left. "Right, Jake?"

"Have I ever been wrong?" Happy talk from off

camera. Then the picture changed to show a grinning fellow with bushy black hair and glasses holding a pointer.

"Not more than half the time." The newscaster smiled. "Here's a chance to redeem yourself. We get a heavy snow every five to ten years, right? You know, more than a foot." Jake was nodding expectantly. "Okay. Try this one: What would happen if it started snowing and didn't stop?"

"For how long, Tom?" Jake cocked his head.

"No, I mean—just never stopped . . ." Tom was frowning in exaggerated earnestness, "indefinitely."

Paul crumpled the empty beer can.

Jake was chuckling, "Sounds like a snow job to me." Boos and groans echoed through the studio. "What we've got right now is plenty. We're beginning to look like Buffalo, New York, during the record-setting winter of '77."

And once again the newscaster: "Jake will explain this crazy weather for you during his forecast a little later in the telecast. Before we look at tonight's other top stories, we'll pause for the following commercial message."

A tabby cat appeared on the screen and started singing in descending notes, "Meow-meow-meow-meow, meow-meow-meow-meow." Then rising in pitch as Paul jumped to his feet, "Meow-meow-meow-meow-meow—" Off the audio. He walked into the kitchen and took another can of beer from the refrigerator. Snapff! After cleaning the top of the can with a paper towel, he tilted some of the cold brew into his mouth and moved to a nearby window.

Manhattan's lights were reflecting on low-pressing clouds, infusing the sky with a yellowish glow, softening and lightening the darkness. Paul's view was restricted by a neighboring building, but he could see that the ground was everywhere white: the alley, the sidewalks, the street—except for a narrowing strip over a steam pipe. Lights in the distance were vague creamy orbs, and below, the street lamp fluttered in a diffuse sphere of gusting white flakes. Then Paul became aware of myriad ashen particles darting unilluminated through the shadows just beyond the glass. The air was alive with snow!

8

~~~~~~

MANHATTAN, ROCKEFELLER CENTER:
11:00 PM, THURSDAY, DECEMBER 21

TEMPERATURE: 27°F

BAROMETER: 29.45″ (FALLING)

WIND: ESE 20–35 MPH

PRECIPITATION: HEAVY SNOW (11″)

FORECAST: SNOW ENDING BY MORNING,
   CLEARING AND COLDER

Paul turned away from the window and tipped up
another mouthful of beer. "Crazy weather," the newscaster had said. How many times in his life had Paul
said that? He had been fascinated by weather for as

long as he could remember. One of his earliest memories was of a tornado that narrowly missed the family home in southern Illinois. Much of the atmosphere's fascination was rooted in its unpredictability—its mystery. The newsman's face replaced that of the cat on the television screen.

Paul Garfield's favorite television program when he was growing up had always been the weather forecasts. His family and old friends were used to it—he was just a weather freak. At least there was plenty of action, unlike friend Charlie's hobby: fossils. No fossil forecasts. Increasing crinoids followed by intermittent ichthyosaurs. New friends were often puzzled upon discovering that his interest in meteorology was serious. Too bad that some people have to feel threatened by difference. He smiled to himself, remembering Amy in high school. She used to get pissed because he would even interrupt their explorations into lovemaking to watch the weather forecast. Couldn't blame her for that. Paul sat down on the edge of his bed. Poquito promptly strutted across the blanket and started pecking at threads on his jeans.

No one was surprised when Paul made the earth's atmosphere his career. Next to the biosphere it was the most dynamic part of nature. Constantly changing. Dynamic and mysterious like the sea, but *more* dynamic and certainly less predictable. Too many variables, the jargon goes. Not amenable to unique modeling. Probably beyond full comprehension on every time scale, Paul decided. Clearly so on the scale of daily changes. Even more so over longer periods: decades, centuries, and millennia. Climates fluctuating as much as the weather. It's "crazy" only because the atmosphere doesn't do what we expect. "Eccentric" is better. Paul sipped his beer.

Mysterious like the spirit of woman. Retaining an elusive detachment, not wanting to be fully understood. And more appealing because of that. A feminine essence of nature. Mother Nature. Father God and Mother Nature. Wonder if they ever made it in bed. Paul grinned, visualizing the slightly pornographic "It's not nice to fool with Mother Nature" poster that had once hung on his office wall. A commercial for mouthwash was playing on the television screen. Paul lit a cigarette. He took a long drag, then began mouthing out unsuccessful smoke rings.

Jake was back on television with the weather. ". . . rate of accumulation tonight—almost two inches per hour—is exceptionally high, equaling that of New York's all-time record snowfall which occurred on the day after Christmas, 1947. Twenty-six inches of snow fell during that storm in less than sixteen hours." Paul stretched out on the bed, head at the lower end, leaning on his elbows.

"Technically, this storm is a northeaster, a coastal storm, and not a blizzard." Jake was looking very serious as he nervously slapped his pointer against the palm of his hand. "A blizzard is defined as having strong winds and low temperatures as well as a lot of snow. Specifically, winds of at least thirty-five miles per hour and temperatures of twenty degrees or less. We are recording gusts as high as thirty-five—even higher in coastal areas—but the steady flow is mostly in the twenties. Fortunately, our temperature is holding at twenty-seven, and we don't expect it to drop much lower until after the clouds clear out early this morning. Of course, it feels much colder because of your wind-chill factor." Paul arched his head back to drain the last of his beer. "The legendary blizzard of 1888," Jake was smiling now, "was a true blizzard. It paralyzed the Northeast with . . ."

The phone rang. The parakeet retreated to its rubber tree in the living room as Paul flipped back to the bedside table. "Hello."

"Hi. It's Howard. Anything new?"

"Yes and no. Talked to Joni. She and friends are trying to help out, but I still haven't heard from Mrs. Conroy. I thought you might be she."

"Okay. Well, I'll get off. Let me know where you stand in the morning."

"I will."

"Boy, this storm is really getting bad. Worst I can remember. We'll have a tough time getting to Vermont tomorrow in any case."

"Let's see what happens. I'll call you early." Paul snubbed out his cigarette.

"Okay. So long."

"Good night, Howard." Back to Jake.

". . . should apologize for not having predicted this snow. But I'm sure the children won't mind. Some snow might even stay on the ground long enough to call it a white Christmas. The storm was a surprise, though. No argument about that. When it moved northeastward into the Atlantic off Cape Hatteras last night, it was a relatively weak surface low with no support aloft, and it was heading out to sea at a normal speed of twenty-five miles per hour. But," raising his pointer for emphasis, "instead, it slowed down and stopped without warning this morning. Since then, the low center has intensified significantly, deepening both at the surface and in the upper atmosphere.

"The storm now extends over an unusually large area and has developed into one of the most vigorous winter storms we've seen in a long time. The latest estimates of barometric pressure at its center are down near twenty-nine inches. That's low for a winter storm this early—most of our really low winter barometers come in February. Some wind gusts over the open ocean have been reported by ships tonight to be as high as seventy-five miles per hour. And that's hurricane velocity."

A shock wave of wind and spray exploded over U.S.S. *Narwhal*, shuddering and rolling the sturdy research ship. Ensign Freehling squeezed a railing on the boat deck and held himself against the pulling, sucking air. It tried to drag him over the side.

Lieutenant Commander Canby lunged, almost falling from the port wing of the bridge into the wheelhouse. "What in hell'd we get into?"

The Second Mate was looking at the continuous-recording anemometer. "The peak is above eighty-three knots. Falling back through fifty now, sir."

"I didn't think we'd hafta worry about anything like that!" gasped Canby. "Anyway, we're driftin' too fast." He took off his cap and wiped his shining forehead with a wrinkled sleeve. "Take 'er off gyropilot, Steve, and head back into that calmer air. Gimme half ahead on one-thirty-five."

"Yes, sir. But . . . sir?"

"Yeah, what?" refitting the cap.

"Those Soviet trawlers are over that way." The boyish navigator smiled hesitantly.

"Aw, to hell with 'em," Canby complained. "How far?"

"Closest is . . ." leaning over a radar scope, "about twelve thousand yards."

"Well, let the bastards get outa our way. We're not gonna capsize on their account. Fuckin' spies." A muted ring sounded as a white light started flashing below a bulkhead telephone.

"That'll be the Commander," predicted the Second Mate. "I figured he'd be rattled out of his bunk by now."

Canby grasped the phone and shouted, "Bridge." He tilted his cap. "Sure was, Cap'n. Over eighty knots. We're movin' back into . . ." He paused to listen. "That's right, no change. Still zero response." Then, "What? The . . . oh, yeah. We sent 'em. Just a second." The portly second officer muffled the mouthpiece with a meaty palm and turned to the navigator, "Got the stats for twenty-three hundred?" Steve quickly handed Canby a length of curling teletype paper. "Here we are, Cap'n . . ." He manipulated it clumsily with his free hand. "Here, ah . . . water temp, air temp, air *pressure* . . . still falling: twenty-eight, seventy-nine. Good God!"

". . . start moving again—if it hasn't already," Jake continued, "so the snow should be tapering off and ending in the metropolitan area within the next couple of hours. Now let's look at the specific forecast." A panel of words and numbers appeared on the television screen. Paul watched the now familiar optimistic predictions once more, then stood up and turned off the set. Clasping hands behind his head, he leaned back to stretch. Time for another beer. He lofted his empty can into a trash bag. Clank!

Two beers later, Paul was slouched on the couch, bare feet propped on the coffee table. His feathered friend was asleep on the rubber tree. He lit a cigarette and sent a stream of smoke rising toward the ceiling. Joni sounded good. She has such a wonderful phone voice: strong but soft, somehow deeper and richer than in person. No other like it. God, it would be good to see her. Have enough time to talk, remember all the good things.

Perhaps the storm is doing me a favor. Howard and I probably won't be able to get to Vermont until at least Saturday. I could postpone that and go to Washington instead. Howard would understand—I'd be checking up on John Conroy, meeting with Senator Bradford. And seeing Joni. Maybe she and I could spend Christmas together. I could call her *now*. His pulse surged. He started to get up. No, better wait till morning. And he sagged back into the couch.

I'd probably act like a nervous jerk—as I did when we had lunch last fall. Why do I always have to learn the hard way? Take things for granted when I have them—no matter how good they are—and let them slip away. Then wake up and want them back desperately when they're gone. It's so self-destructive.

Paul took another drag on his cigarette, tried another smoke ring. Hey, a good one. A pale-white doughnut shivered out over his feet. It looked as though it was turning slightly to the left. He wondered if he could induce spinning by twisting his mouth at the last moment. He tried it. No good; shapeless puffs. Then it worked. A thick, fuzzy ring with a small hole—but rotating very slowly counterclockwise. Cyclonic circulation. No spiral arms, but it had an eye.

Funny how this winter storm has squatted and built up in one spot. I wonder what the basis is for predicting its time of renewed movement. They didn't know it was going to stop in the first place. Be nice to see a few satellite photos—should be one on the tube in the morning. Paul started listing on his fingers the various satellites he knew that could provide a good view: polar-orbit satellites, oblique-orbit satellites, equatorial satellites.

Let's see, which of the hovering vehicles could give the best angle? He nervously tapped ashes into the beanbag ashtray nestled on the arm of the sofa. That Cosmos the Russians put over Colombia last spring would be good. And the other six; those two series intersect right over the storm center. Ironic. They're in the best position. . . . He stiffened and sat straight. His ash tray spilled on the floor. The May Day intersection! All those trawlers!

Suddenly he was standing, rubbing the back of his head. His heart pounded in his ear. Conroy quit the project Tuesday, disappeared yesterday. Was it because . . . could the cause have been emergency duty? Of course! Why didn't that sink in sooner? How can I . . . Conroy must've said something to Jane about his schedule. Dropped some hint about the suddenness of his decision to quit. Paul moved to the phone. He punched the Conroys' number and waited. Nothing happened. He waited. Finally there were clicking noises: "I'm sorry, the number you are calling is temporarily out of service. I'm sorry . . ."

9

~~~~~~

WASHINGTON NATIONAL AIRPORT: MID-
NIGHT, THURSDAY/FRIDAY, DECEMBER
21/22

TEMPERATURE: 27° F

BAROMETER: 28.29" (FALLING)

WIND: NE 25–40 MPH

PRECIPITATION: HEAVY SNOW (17")

FORECAST: SNOW ENDING BY MORNING,
CLEARING AND COLDER

Admiral Zimber's head drooped, chins piling up on
his full chest. He had settled himself at one end of
the gray velvet couch in his Pentagon office to wait.

To wait for a change to better news. He clutched a tilting tumbler half filled with bourbon and water. Floating in it were three rounded remnants of ice cubes. Fatigued by anxiety and relaxed by alcohol, he had fallen asleep. The Admiral's breathing was slow and deep, periodically palpitating his lips. A muscle spasm distorted the left side of his sagging face and . . .

Frigid air prickled his reddened cheeks and moistened his eyes as he trudged onto the frozen lake. "Ah-huh, looks like a good target," Zimber assured himself, puffing plumes of fog.

He stopped and turned to his right—that enormous red spruce; then around to the left—and over there the moose. Strange and familiar landmarks on the shore. "Close to the same place as last year." Wiping his eye with a bulky gloved fist, he dropped a pick and spade to mark his claim. Then, twisting and muttering, he wrestled one arm from under a strap of his pack basket and triumphantly swung his burden to the ice.

He glanced up at the thick gray sky as he removed his sheepskin glove and reached into a coat pocket. "Sure as hell feels like snow." He pulled out a leather-covered pint flask. "Be just as well. Always brings luck." He looked down and unscrewed the cap with a grunt. "At ease, Jim. First order's a visit with Jim," and he tilted up a mouthful of Mr. Beam's fortification.

After stuffing the bottle safely into his pack, he stooped over to recover his pick. "Well, ahhh," taking a full breath, "I estimate we'll have to go through about ten inches, maybe a foot." With that, he planted his lug boots nearly three feet apart and grasped the pick at the end of its handle with his left hand, flush under its head with the right. Spitting on the ice as a starting signal, he let fly.

Chonk! Chonk! Chank! The heavy steel point plunged in again and again, powdering and shattering the ice. After eleven strokes he paused, already sweating freely. His arctic coat was comfortable when he was sitting still icefishing, but it was overinsulated for strenuous work. He jerked his head to one side, held his breath. What the hell's that noise? Can't be a motor launch. He looked over his left shoulder. Well for Christ's sake, that's a new one. A dark-haired young lady in a pink ski suit was manhandling a chain saw. "Wonder who she's working for. Better keep the hell away from my hole."

When she started to cut, ice dust sprayed up into a white fan ten feet high. That led Zimber to notice the falling snow: bright spots which seemed to vanish just before alighting—as though they were reflections from countless moving mirrors. Beyond the girl stood the moose, looking much heavier and hairier through the snow.

Returning to his project, the Admiral bent forward, bracing hand on knee, and scooped and brushed ice chips out of the pit. "Oughta be gettin' down to water." Next he retrieved the spade and, with heavy foot-pushing, proceeded to widen his excavation. He was about to renew the attack with his pick when he heard the blatting grumble of an ill-muffled diesel engine. Pssshh! Pssshh! Air brakes.

He swiveled around to his left and, sure enough, a square truck tractor at the front of a flatbed trailer had just come to a halt a good hundred yards out on the frozen lake. "Holy shit, they'd better be damn sure of secure ice." Half a dozen men were scurrying around under a small crane unloading what appeared to be lengths of steel superstructure. The girl with the chain saw was gone. "Must've gotten the word to steer clear of me. Scared her off." The big hairy moose was sniffing the air. Partially screened by snow spots, it seemed to have quite a long snout, sort of a semi-trunk.

Chong! Chonk! Chink! Thunk. Zimber leaned the pick against his leg, then dragged a glove over his dripping forehead. "Shit! Must be in nearly a foot 'n' a half. Where in hell's the lake?" He glanced around at the truck. The crew had almost completed construction of a derrick-type structure. It looked for all the world like an oil rig. "Are they gonna drill into this ice? Nosy bastards! Better consult Jim."

He tromped over to the pack basket and withdrew his whiskey. After arching backward for a hearty swig, he turned to watch the drilling rig. Platform power humming, drill stem turning. "Probably some goddam reporters." Then he looked toward the shore. "Mother of God! That's no moose. It's a woolly elephant. Got curly tusks." Zimber could see the beast more clearly as it plodded deliberately out onto the ice. "Well, shit. Watching wildlife isn't gonna get me my hole."

This time he sank the pick sixteen times before scraping and spading. The funnel-shaped pit looked almost three feet deep. "Fuckin' lake must be frozen solid." He was determined to get in some fishing. Couldn't face his father without a good mess. Now more truck noise. A blue diesel tractor emerged from around the point behind the red spruce. As he watched, three trailers in tandem came into view.

The caravan rolled all the way to the center of the lake, where it finally stopped. Another word with Jim. He wiped his ruddy, whiskery face with a swipe of his sleeve. A large table or platform had been erected in front of the trailers. On either side was a big box of some sort. A lot of people were moving back and forth placing cages or . . . stools? No, foldup chairs.

"Hey, pal. Got a match?"

Zimber wheeled around. There stood a tan, sinewy man wearing an aluminum hard hat, purple sweatshirt pulled back to the elbows, and striped overalls. His expression conveyed the sensitivity of a leather mask. "Match?" he repeated, sticking a cigarette into the crack of his mouth. There was a tattooed whirlwind on his muscular forearm.

"Sure," voiced Zimber with bridled eagerness. "I'll have a cigar m' self." He unzipped his coat partway and reached into his shirt pocket. "You from the CIA?" He raised the pick head like a torch and frictioned a kitchen match across it.

"Nope," sucking the flame. "Pushin' pipe down that drill hole." His slight nod meant thank you.

"Oh? You some kind of investigator?"

"Nope. Iceman."

The Admiral tensed. "I'll tell you what, the ice is sure thick this year." Zimber's eyes were smarting in cigar smoke.

The man with the hard hat squinted in the direction of the crowd gathering around the trailers. "Yeah, we're into it ten thousand feet already." He tipped his helmet forward and scratched the back of his head, groaning as if painfully constipated. His cigarette was squeezed between clenched teeth that were fully exposed like those of a chimpanzee preparing to scream. The itch relieved, he looked at the Admiral. "Goin' to the concert?" The questioner's shining black eyes rounded to the intensity of a ferret in stalk.

"What concert?" Zimber rotated his cigar a couple of times in his mouth, then sank his teeth into it. "I'm gonna do some fishin'."

"New Wisconsin Rock Concert," with a slight head motion toward the growing congregation seated near lake center. At that moment the vibrant throbbing of electronic bass amplified into the atmosphere.

"I don't go for that hippie rock bullshit," and the Admiral spat out some cigar juice.

"Great new group: Flaky Finish." The stranger was now moving to the beat with the loose, disjointed wiggling-wobbling of a marionette. "They really needle through. Chil-ly *space!*"

"Admiral!" Zimber thought he heard someone call him.

Iceman was shuffling erratically in his snowpacs. "Come on, man. The sound is called 'crystal rock.'" The air was electric with pulsing bass. Descending snow spots brightened in sympathy with the beat. Even the ice seemed to be thumping, pounding.

"Admiral!" There it was again. Zimber looked to his left.

His mouth fell open. The cigar butt bounced off his stomach as he gasped, "Whaa . . . huuh!" The betusked behemoth was rolling and shaking its hairy high-humped head as it galloped, thundering toward the Admiral in full charge.

The immense pachyderm's trunk rose through

great coils of ivory to flash a mammoth red maw that mouthed, "Zimber!"

Everything was jostling, but the Admiral was paralyzed in terror. "Zimber! Come on, Admiral. Wake up!" And he slowly realized that he was returning from sleep.

The worried face of Walter Popowski. Gradually the Admiral regained control of his limbs. He looked around his office. The door was closed. The wall clock showed 12:20. Popowski was holding the glass of bourbon. As Zimber's memory revived and his consciousness became full, he suffered a new surge of panic.

Rising unsteadily, he felt hot and sticky. He swiveled his face toward Popowski. "Are they here?"

"Yes, sir. In the outer office."

"Good. Give me a minute," lumbering toward the bathroom. "Fix me a drink, will you?" he shouted before slamming the door. Popowski opened a cabinet beneath the bookcases to expose a small coppertone refrigerator. From it he removed a bottle of bourbon and a small bucket of ice cubes. Walter Popowski was tall and thin with straight gray hair. The former Rear Admiral looked pale and tired. After pouring water from the silver decanter on the Admiral's desk, Popowski returned the bottle and ice to the refrigerator. He wiped his wet hand on the pants of his gray-flannel suit.

Zimber marched out of the bathroom, mopping his face with a black towel. He dropped into his desk chair, which squeaked. Looking off toward the window, he spoke almost in a whisper. "Bring 'em in."

Popowski opened the door to the outer office and announced, "The Admiral is ready."

Two well-groomed men in their thirties preceded him into the inner chamber. Popowski closed the door as Zimber waved the newcomers to the couch. His intense dark eyes fixed the two civilians. At length he began, "What I want to know first is," enunciating crisply but quietly as though questioning frightened children, "*could* it be due to Soviet interference?"

Before either of the younger men was ready to reply, Popowski pointed out, "We have no evidence of any activity other than monitoring by their satellites and a couple of trawlers."

"Yes, I know. You already gave me your information, Mr. Popowski." The Admiral's voice was increasing in volume and trembled slightly. "Now do you mind if I hear from these gentlemen who have just made a difficult journey through the snow at midnight?" He paused, then turned back to the others. "Which one of you is Berger?"

The one on the right, a tall Black man wearing a plaid shirt under his jacket, finally answered, "He didn't come. I'm George Williams. This is Don Panella. We're his co-workers. He asked us to come in his place."

Looking somewhat perplexed, Zimber clasped hands in front of his chin and leaned forward on his elbows. "But I asked for *his* report."

"He felt that he couldn't . . . shouldn't leave," Williams continued. "He wants to keep on top of the situation without interruption. He said he'd be happy to report to you on the phone."

"Aaach!" The Admiral jerked his head. "Too risky. You don't realize what's at stake here. The interior of this office I *know* is clean. But I don't trust *anything* that goes outside. Anyway, what about the Russians?"

"The most honest thing we can say," Panella offered, "is that we don't know. *Narwhal* detects nothing now, but we don't really know what those trawlers and subs might have done last summer."

"*Narwhal* detects nothing *now!* Hell, it's a little late to be looking, isn't it?" Zimber was beginning to shout. "*They were out there in July!*" He stood up and walked around to the front of the desk, taking a gulp of the drink Popowski had made for him. Then he asked in a very low voice, "Any changes?"

"No, sir," answered Williams.

"No response at *all?*" in rising volume.

"None."

Suddenly Zimber wheeled. "Goddam it to *hell!*" He crashed his right fist down on the desk, sloshing the drink in his other hand. "I was told that we were absolutely safe!"

"Nothing is absolute, Admiral," observed Popowski.

Zimber scowled. "Spare me your ninth-grade profundities." He stalked back behind the desk and sank into his chair. After another swallow of booze and a deep breath, he spoke more calmly. "I guess the only thing to do is forget the mistakes and get out of this as quickly as possible." He looked at Popowski, "What time did the emergency plan go into effect?"

"About twenty-one hundred hours." Walter was leaning against the bookcases. "We've got Rodek; he's on his way back to New London." Popowski straightened up. "The bathyscaphe's new captain, Duncan Smith, is already there, and *Nessie* is being fitted in the hold of the mother ship, *Manatee*. With luck, they'll put to sea by oh eight hundred."

Zimber got up again and walked to the window. He peeked through the blinds at the snow outside. "Incredible." Then he turned to Williams and Panella. "You must've had a hell of a time getting here. It took me two hours earlier this evening."

"We did," Williams replied. "Our jeep got stuck twice in drifts."

Panella added, "I guess we're going back in a snow-plow."

"Both of you are going?" Zimber asked accusingly.

"Yes, sir," said Williams.

"Oh, no. No, no, no," waving a finger. "Walter," he faced Popowski, "I thought I told you I wanted at least one of their men here at all times?"

"Yes, sir, but I haven't had a chance to pass that on yet."

"Well, I'll pass it on right now. Panella, you stay. Williams, when you get back, tell Berger to send somebody else down here with an update to replace Panella. I've ordered two snow vehicles—one for backup. We'll have continuous round trips as this thing develops so that my office is kept current. No radio and no phones! Right? Only in case of emergency when there's no other choice . . . and then in NI"—Naval Intelligence—"yellow code. We can't afford any leaks. Not any!"

The Admiral abruptly marched to his bookcases, then stooped and opened the refrigerator cabinet to get his bottle. Returning to his desk, he poured himself another drink and immediately swallowed some. "If your great team hadn't screwed up, we wouldn't be in this mess."

"Look, Admiral," Williams asserted, "we didn't screw up. Unless it's the Russians, then we don't

97

know what's wrong. and if it is them, we don't know how."

"Young man, that is what I call screwing the hell *up!*" Zimber swallowed again, then placed both hands on his desk top and leaned forward. "Gentlemen. I don't mean to be unreasonable." He sighed. "Understand that I'm under tremendous pressure."

"Yes, sir," replied Panella without expression.

"Good. Now if you'll wait in the outer office for a few minutes . . ." The Admiral nodded at Popowski, who promptly ushered the others out and returned, closing the door.

"What's the security situation?" Zimber demanded of his assistant.

"Some questions from outside scientists are beginning to filter through." Popowski was pacing across the floor in front of the desk. "And there have been a couple of suggestions that something abnormal is going on. But . . ." He stopped and looked up. "We've been able to squelch them pretty effectively so far. God knows what others we'll be getting."

"Well, we'll be ready if it comes to that. Those fuckin' Russians." He half smiled. "Never could trust 'em."

"We may have another problem." Popowski was pacing again and staring at the carpet, holding hands behind his back.

"Well?" The Admiral was looking out the window again.

"Garfield may get involved in more than Conroy's disappearance."

"Like what?"

"Senator Bradford called him tonight and asked to meet him as soon as he can get to Washington."

"Holy shit!" Zimber let go of the cord, and the blinds crashed down. For a moment he was silent. Then he turned abruptly. "Bring Garfield here. We'll have a believer one way or the other."

"That's easier said than done with these weather conditions," Walter offered.

"Look, I don't care if you tie him to a tractor and plow all the way. Get *him!*"

10

〰〰〰〰〰〰〰〰〰〰〰〰〰〰〰〰〰〰

MANHATTAN, ROCKEFELLER CENTER:
MIDNIGHT, THURSDAY/FRIDAY,
DECEMBER 21/22

TEMPERATURE: 27°F

BAROMETER: 29.41″ (FALLING)

WIND: ESE 20–40 MPH

PRECIPITATION: HEAVY SNOW (13″)

FORECAST: SNOW ENDING BY MORNING,
CLEARING AND COLDER

Have to get to Washington as soon as possible. But
how? Paul Garfield was standing at his bedroom window, watching the snowstorm. Forty minutes wasted

on the phone: There's no public transportation, can't charter anything. By sea is the only way. And it must be rough as hell.

"Heavy snow and high winds have completely immobilized New York City," stated the tinny transistor speaker. "Even subway service has been greatly reduced. Those trains that are operating are experiencing delays and are unable to maintain regular schedules. The inability of employees to get to work, overcrowding, several accidents—one with serious injury—a power failure, and the shortage of law-enforcement personnel to control vandalism, muggings, and assaults are among the reasons cited for the declining service.

"Very shortly," the radio voice continued, "we expect an announcement that all subway service has been suspended until morning. Even then, some trains may have great difficulty in turning around and re-entering the city. The Mayor has asked all persons to stay where they are tonight and not attempt to travel." Paul snapped the radio off in frustration.

He surveyed West 86th Street below him. How could he get to a ship even if one were available? The street was clogged with snow; no traffic was moving. Almost none—something was rounding the corner. He heard faint motor noises as a dark form darted by. What was that? A snowmobile! Paul fairly jumped away from the window and flopped across his bed as Poquito flew around the room screeching in alarm. Seizing the phone, Paul punched out numbers.

"*Hal*-oh."

"Howard, Paul."

"Hi, Paul. What's the latest—besides the storm? It just keeps getting worse."

"Listen, Howard, I need your help. It's extremely important."

"Lay it on me."

"I need transportation as soon as possible, and nothing's running. Can you give me a lift on your snowmobile?"

"Well . . . yeah, I guess so . . . if it's that important. We might've been out on the trail in Vermont by now anyway. Where we going?"

"I don't know yet."

"Huh?"

"I mean, I'll tell you when you get here. How soon can you pick me up?"

"What time ya got? You're not stoned, are you?"

"Twelve-forty. Unfortunately not."

"Well, gimme an hour. Maybe less. Let's say one-thirty."

"I'll be downstairs. This means a lot, Howard."

"Okay. See ya."

Paul hung up and meandered into the living room. The lesser problem was solved. Now he could get to a ship—if only he had a ship to get to. He harbored no hope of obtaining a private boat. Even if he were able to find someone willing to attempt the trip—which would be unlikely before daylight—he had no way to make or guarantee immediate payment. The quickest way would be on a U.S. ship, one already in the Port of New York. Paul stroked a book match to ignition and lit a cigarette.

His best hope lay with contacts in NASA, the National Aeronautics and Space Administration. They'd have more clout with bureaucrats than David Bradford. Chris Gonn might be able to help. Paul's old friend and one-time boss, Christopher Gonn, was now

Director of Orbital Intelligence-Vehicle Evaluation (OI-VE). But Gonn had moved and probably had a new unlisted phone number. John Conroy would've had the current one. And Jane could probably find it if Paul were only able to call her. Zimber's boys must've killed her phone. Well, stop worrying and start trying. There must be some way to reach Chris.

The parakeet had settled on the rubber tree. As Paul sat down on the couch next to the living-room phone the bird flew toward him. When the phone rang, Poquito doubled back to safety. Again Paul hoped that the call was from Jane. "Hello?"

"Is Maria there?" asked a man.

"You must have the wrong number."

"Sorry."

Paul stared at the phone for several seconds after hanging up. He frowned and took a long drag on his cigarette. "Poqui, I don't like the feel of that. I should've taken Jane's comments seriously. My phone's probably bugged too." He rose and strode rapidly back into the bedroom. "I think I'd better vacate the premises. You'll be on your own for a while, little friend."

Despite the hour and the weather, the phone booth on Amsterdam Avenue was occupied. Two persons waiting to use it were huddled on the downwind side. Probably had no way to get home. Paul moved in behind them to form a triangle of bodies. He was much more appropriately dressed than the others in his down parka, goggles, heavy gloves, and rubber snow boots. They were obviously chilled. He looked away when they squinted up at him. An ageless Oriental man and a heavyset, red-faced woman wrapped in a green shawl.

Snow was blowing from the east in a blinding torrent. The wind must be a steady twenty-five knots, Paul guessed. He waited and watched. Street lights faded quickly through the milky continuum. Progressively farther away they dimmed into invisibility: primordial emissions from unimaginably distant stars. He peered upward. It was impossible to see just how low the clouds were; the moving mass of snow obscured the sky. The storm showed no signs of abating. Indeed, it seemed to be continually worsening. Becoming extremely dangerous. Something very serious must be wrong. That son of a bitch Zimber. He wouldn't care unless his own skin were at stake. Maybe the Russians outsmarted the bastard. Got to get on the phone. Jesus, hurry up. Maybe, I . . .

The body in the booth lunged out into the wind. A huge man with streaming white hair and wrapped in a great bathrobelike overcoat. The Oriental man, seeming tiny by comparison, darted inside and slammed the door. Paul moved closer to the lady. She was shivering. "Ain't this awful?" she rasped. He nodded and put his arm around her shoulders. In most places the snow was more than a foot deep on the sidewalk and in the street. Drifts up to several feet deep curved around or reached behind obstructions, following the wind; it swept wisps and wavering streamers of snow along their crests. A drift walling off the street side of the phone booth was almost three feet high.

Looking through the glass of the booth, Paul watched the large man in black rapidly disappear into the blowing snow. Then there was another dark shape. It seemed to be growing larger, to be moving toward the booth. It was low to the ground; Paul supposed it must be a dog, but it didn't move like a dog. Very slow—sort of crawling. Jesus Christ, a man!

Paul rushed around the booth and over to the figure that was advancing on hands and knees through the snow, away from the wind. The old black man was shuddering uncontrollably. Paul thrust gloved hands under the man's armpits and lifted him to unsteady feet. The old man put his bare right hand on Paul's shoulder for support. There was a strong smell of cheap wine. The man's clothing gave him little protection: blue skullcap, old Army fatigue jacket. One of his shoes had no sole. After considerable swaying and struggling, Paul managed to zip the old man into his parka. "Here, put on these gloves." There was an entrance to an apartment building a few doors down. "We've got a short walk," Paul shouted. "Let's go." The wind gusted, and Paul was instantly cold without his coat. Snow particles felt sharp.

The outer lobby was heated and had a marble bench. Paul helped the old man seat himself. "Do you have any place to go?" The other said nothing. He just sat there trembling and staring into Paul's eyes. "You wait here. I've got to use the phone. I'll be back in a few minutes." From the corner of his eye, Paul could see the doorman inside waving at him. The inner door opened. He looked Indian.

"Oh, mister. You cannot leave that man here."

"The hell I can't. He's freezing. I'll be right back." Avoiding the trap of an argument, Paul opened the door just far enough to slip through and leaned out into the wind. The lady with the green shawl was inside the booth, but two other persons were now in line. "Oh no. Goddammit!"

As Paul approached, the lady beckoned to him and opened the door. "I'm done," she said. "I saw ya comin' back so I held it for ya." She turned to the newcomers and shouted, "He was next."

Paul nodded and patted her on the back. "Thank you very much."

Her face opened into an enormous smile of crooked teeth. "You're cert'iny welcome, gorgeous. Now get yourself in there out of this wind."

He nervously wrestled some coins and a little address book from his pants pocket. First he tried the number for Christopher Gonn's old residence, but he was sure it wouldn't be right. "Credit-card call," he told the operator and recited his number. Gonn's former number rang, but Paul quickly learned that it now belonged to someone else.

He knew that his colleague was still in Greenbelt, Maryland. The address had been on the envelope of Gonn's Christmas card. Next he tried Directory Assistance: "I'm sorry, that is an unpublished number."

"Thank you." Shit! Time for Plan B.

Margie Sampson was a close friend of Chris's; she'll know his number. "No, Paul, I haven't seen Chris in a couple of years. I'm not sure if I could even find his old number. Say, you sound great. When are you coming to town?"

"Listen, Margie. This is urgent. Can you think of any way to get his current number?"

There was a pause, then, "Yes, I think so. I know a girl who's been dating him a lot lately. Can you stay there for a minute? I'll try to get it and call you right back."

"Okay. Please hurry. Here's my number," and he read her the digits on the face of the phone box, then hung up to wait. In the rush and excitement of calling, he hadn't felt the cold. Now he did. He rubbed his hands, flexed his fingers. Without the parka, his upper body was covered only by a light-blue shirt. A draft through the crack at the door gave him goose bumps. He took a pack of cigarettes from his pocket. Come on, Margie. Rap! Rap! Rap! An old woman was hitting the glass with an umbrella handle and glowering at him. He touched his watch and held up two fingers. There were three persons waiting outside now. God, they must be miserable. He lit a cigarette, exhaled slowly. Check the time: 1:03. Less than half an hour to meet Howard. Come on, Margie.

Paul's left hand was holding down the receiver. At the first sound of the ring, he yanked it to his ear. "Margie?"

"Uh-huh. I'll tell you, it took more than a little convincing to get Chris's number out of her. I told her to have him phone you, but she didn't want to do that. Anyway, here's the number. Ready?"

"Shoot." He wrote it down on the inside cover of his match book. "Thank you, thank you, Margie. You're a lifesaver. Buy you a drink next chance we get."

"Promises, promises. Make it soon. You can help dig me out."

"Okay." Rap! Rap! Rap! "Gotta go now. Take care, and thanks again." He turned toward the old woman's cursing scowl and held up his index finger. One more call. He punched the buttons. His finger

107

slipped. Again. Number please be right. Chris, please be home.

In a moment, Gonn was on. "Trust me, Chris. I do not exaggerate when I tell you that this is urgent—a matter of national security. And it is literally getting worse by the minute." His voice was precise and dramatic. Gonn could tell that Paul was convinced of what he was saying. "Pull whatever strings are necessary, Chris. Hell, tell them it's a national emergency— it *is*—that I'm indispensable . . . anything. But absolutely avoid the Pentagon. Okay?"

"Loud and clear, Paul. I have a friend pretty high in Transportation. I'll try the Coast Guard. Call me back in fifteen minutes."

"Please get it done, Chris. I can't overstate its importance." The moment he hung up, the old woman with the umbrella started pushing in the door. He couldn't stay there. He remembered a bar two blocks down, and hoped it was open.

The old man in the outer lobby had stopped shivering. "Feeling better?" Paul asked. The other looked up and nodded. "If you're warming up in here, I'll take back my coat and gloves." The old man nodded again. The doorman in his brown-and-gold uniform was watching from the inner foyer. The parka felt magnificently warm around Paul's cold shoulders as he zipped it all the way up.

At the door he looked back and held up his hand for goodbye. God knows how many are as bad off as or worse off than the old man, how many will die if this storm doesn't stop.

The onrushing snow was as thick as he had ever seen. Choking the wind, burying the ground. Walking was an ordeal. Drifts up to five feet deep trailed

108

across the pavements like migrating white dunes. Cars were abandoned in the streets. Visibility was nearly zero into the wind, less than ten yards away from it. Paul's goggles allowed him to see that much. The snow stung his cheeks. He saw only one other person. Apparently people were taking the warnings seriously and staying home. Perhaps the bar would be closed. He had to find another phone; he couldn't trust his own.

The outside of the bar was dark. It looked closed. Depressed and pessimistic, Paul trudged toward the door. As he approached, it swung open and out pushed a policeman in a long navy-blue coat. "Is the place open, officer?"

"Are you kiddin'? It's like St. Patrick's Day in there. They're talking about stayin' open all night 'cause a lotta people are stranded."

Paul started in, then turned. "Say, officer."

"Yeah, what?"

"I found an old man in the snow—put him in a building entrance. Is there some place for him near here? Any shelters or . . ."

"Nah, not right around here. What is he, a wino?"

"I guess so. Can you help him? He'll freeze if he has to stay outside."

"Only thing I could do is take him to the Precinct. Pretty damn full in there already."

"He's in the lobby of an apartment building. Two blocks up, first one down from the phone booth." Paul was shouting in the wind. "Will you check on him?" The policeman nodded, and Paul went inside.

The lounge was crowded and chaotic. It *was* like St. Patrick's Day . . . or the night the lights went out. An atmosphere of celebration and liberation. It reminded Paul of a hurricane party he had survived once in the Florida Keys. People obviously enjoy a mild, temporary emergency. So long as it *is* mild and temporary, he thought. Everyone seems to understand that normal rules of conduct are suspended. Outrageous circumstances: outrageous behavior. So long as neither is too outrageous.

It was a wild scene—the jukebox alternately thundering and screaming, a mass of people pulsing to the beat, a crowd five deep along the bar, and everyone trying to make himself heard. The noise level was so high that Paul wondered if he would be able to hear anything on the phone—if he could even get downstairs. The clock above the bottles showed 1:14. Almost time to call Gonn back. There wasn't time to go anywhere else. At least the people here might believe that he had to make an emergency call, and be relaxed enough not to care if he asked to butt in. He wriggled his way to the bar and, by waving a five-dollar bill and yelling, finally managed to secure a cognac. Paul cradled the snifter in both hands and inhaled the searing fumes.

He overheard the man on his right shouting to a burly companion, ". . . an' then he says to fuzzy ol' Jake, 'What if it never quits?' Hah-haa!"

"Well, I'll be go ta hell."

Paul swallowed some brandy and smiled to himself with watering eyes. It took three minutes for him to work his way through the crowd and down the stairs to where two phone booths stood outside the restrooms. It was 1:20, time to call. Luckily, one of the booths was just being vacated, and no one else was waiting. Paul called Gonn, but the line was busy. Seated inside, he opened the booth door for air and lit a cigarette. He savored a sip of cognac. He would probably be late for Howard. Then he remembered the call for "Maria." What if Howard were intercepted? Paul immediately called him. The phone rang and rang: no answer. With luck he was on his way.

Paul tried Gonn again: still busy. He sighed. Hope Jane's okay. And John . . . could she possibly have been right about him? I should've known the lines would be tapped. Maybe by now I'm being followed. Somebody at the outside phone booth? No. Again he called Chris Gonn. *Still* busy. "Jesus, come on," he whispered impatiently.

There was fairly heavy traffic to and from the restrooms, but the noise was much less than it was upstairs. A pretty girl with curly black hair and a low neckline surged out of the ladies' lounge. She spied Paul and sauntered over in her clinging red dress. "Hi, bashful. You hidin' in there?" Before he could answer, she leaned in and licked his mouth. He backed into the corner, hoisting his cognac out of the way, and she immediately straddled his knee. "Relax, honey."

"I've got to make a call. Really . . . I'll see you later." She dismounted with exaggerated indignation and strutted off. He took another drag, put down his cognac, and called once more. This time it rang.

"Hello." Gonn's voice.

"Hello, Chris. It's Paul. Any news?"

"I think we've got it done. What's that racket?"

"I'm in a bar. I'll close the door." Paul was excited. "How'd you work it? What do I do?"

"Coast Guard cutter. Their pier in lower Manhattan at three A.M. Got a pencil?"

"Go ahead," and Paul wrote down the details.

111

"At thirty knots, you should be up the Potomac early tomorrow afternoon, but it'll be a hell of a rough ride. Gale winds most of the way. You're sure you don't want to try something else?"

"There *isn't* anything else." Paul was emphatic.

"Okay. You expecting opposition?"

"Don't know, Chris. Maybe."

"I'll have somebody meet you. The arrangements may leak."

"Yeah . . . that's right," Paul sighed.

"How about you 'ex'? For press protection."

"Okay. I'll call her, Chris, but I don't have much time."

"Let me help—save you a little."

"Good. I'll just tell her I'm coming."

"And I'll fill in the details. We'll get you a welcoming party. Now you'd better get going." After Paul gave him Joni's number, Gonn wished Paul luck and they hung up.

Almost 1:30. "Hey, fella." A man was speaking to him. "You gonna be offa that soon? I gotta call home. I'm gonna be late. Too fuckin' much schnow." The man's white shirt was untucked and hung down from his protruding stomach.

"Last one," Paul assured him.

And in a moment Joni was saying, "Jane Conroy called me from a neighbor's house. She said her phone wasn't working." Joni sounded wide awake. "I told her what we're doing. Did David call you?"

"Yes, he did. Joni, this is extremely serious. I don't have time to explain. Chris Gonn of NASA will call you later. I need your help. I'm coming to Washington today on an urgent mission, and I may be in some danger."

"What can I do?"

"Meet me. Pick me up. Chris will help you. In this kind of situation you can't trust anyone, so please keep it *absolutely* confidential. I've spoken only to Chris Gonn and you."

"Where will you be? How on earth are you going to get here? We've got a foot and a half of snow with drifts over your head."

"Chris will tell you. Please be there. Figure something. Now I've got to go."

"I'll do my damnedest. Maybe I'll ski."

It was 1:33. Paul shouldered his way through the teeming lounge and plunged out into the blast of snow. He broke into a trot but didn't seem to gain much speed. The snow was too deep. It was like trying to run in loose sand. Much effort, little result. Fast becoming winded, he settled into a slogging walk. He would be home in five minutes, ten minutes late for Howard. Would Howard be there . . . or would someone else? Paul wished that he had phoned Howard from outside and arranged to meet him somewhere else.

11

〰〰〰〰〰〰〰〰〰〰〰〰〰〰〰〰〰

MANHATTAN, ROCKEFELLER CENTER:
  1:00 AM, FRIDAY, DECEMBER 22

  TEMPERATURE: 26°F

  BAROMETER: 29.37″ (FALLING)

  WIND: 25–40 MPH

  PRECIPITATION: HEAVY SNOW (15″)

  FORECAST: SNOW ENDING BY MORNING,
    CLEARING AND COLDER

Howard wasn't there. Apparently he hadn't arrived
yet. At least Paul couldn't see any snowmobile tracks.
Of course, they could have been obliterated in
minutes by the sweeping snow. Paul's watch showed

1:42 as he stomped up to the apartment building. He glanced nervously around, then stepped back out of the light. The canvas canopy was flapping rapidly. Howard would've waited longer than this. Maybe he had been held up and phoned while Paul was out. Maybe the storm was too . . . At that moment Paul became conscious of a new sound. Through the whistling rush of the wind and the flap-flap-flapping of the canopy rose motor noise. Louder. Growling like a chain saw, or an outboard, or . . . a snowmobile! Howard Tannenbaum's big yellow-and-black machine emerged from the billowing snow and whined down to an idle at Paul's feet. The label BLIZZARD identified it as a racing model.

"Sorry I'm late," Howard shouted, smiling out of his goggles and hood. "Took an hour after all." He climbed off and embraced Paul, giving him an enthusiastic and athletic greeting of backslapping and jostling. Howard was clearly exhilarated by this rare adventure in the middle of the night. He was a large, gangling man whose movements seemed jerky and disjointed. In a former life he might have been a Great Dane. He was clean-shaven, but the roots of his heavy black beard shadowed the lower half of his face in charcoal gray. He lifted his goggles and squinted at Paul. "Know where we're goin' yet?"

"Lower Manhattan. Coast Guard pier next to Battery Park."

"By the Staten Island ferry?"

"Uh-huh. Near there."

"Has this to do with Conroy?" Howard's upper lip rose quizzically.

"I'd better tell you later. Let's get out of here, okay?"

115

Howard swallowed, then grinned. "I guess it's gotta be." He straddled the snowmobile seat and Paul climbed on behind. Paul wondered what his friend's reaction would be if he knew that Paul was on his way to Washington. He'd probably offer to drive him there on his snow machine. It would certainly be shorter overland, and could be a lot quicker if the storm let up. But with the visibility approaching zero, it would be suicidal unless one knew every detail of the route. A chilling and perhaps fitting fate: buried in a snowbank or sinking to the bottom of a river.

Paul shouted in Howard's ear. "What do you think, Henry Hudson?"

"Nah, let's try Broadway." r-r-r-r-R-R-R-R-RRRR! Hunching behind the windshield, they accelerated into the swarming snowflakes and roared westward across Columbus Avenue.

"Hey, how come you didn't turn left?" Paul yelled, holding on tightly.

"We'll go down Amsterdam," hollered Howard.

"Wrong way."

"That'll be better. We can see the lights coming."

"Yeah, just before they hit us." And they swept south onto Amsterdam Avenue. Howard had to go much more slowly than he would have liked because of the minimal visibility. Repeatedly he had to swerve to avoid collisions with abandoned cars. The dark and bright contrasts of city night were awash in white, but the pulsing glimmer of street lamps penetrated the snow from both sides and kept him on the right general course. Like runway lights through a fog: eerie and full of warning. He tried to steer down the middle. He had seen no moving vehicles.

Headlights! Massive object! A Department of Sani-

116

tation garbage truck, snowplow blade scraping toward them. They turned sharply to the right to avoid it and had to lean far in that direction to keep from tipping over. Shoving past them, the ponderous white tortoise was engaged in a hopeless enterprise. The streaming snow covered and drifted its path in seconds. Nonetheless, Howard took advantage of the smoother surface in the wake of the truck.

Inside their parka hoods, the two could hear little above the muffling grumble of their snowmobile motor and the swirling whine of the wind. Paul wasn't sure whether he had first heard the other motor or seen the shape and color, but he was suddenly aware that a black-and-green snowmobile was paralleling them on the right. He jabbed Howard and motioned with his thumb. Howard nodded, then bobbed his head toward the left. There was a second dark machine on that side; its driver was thrusting downward with his arm, ordering Howard to halt. Paul shouted to his friend, "Got a flashlight?"

"Tool pouch," came the reply over Howard's shoulder. Paul pulled it out and turned the beam on the driver to his right. "Who the hell are those guys?" asked Howard.

The illuminated interloper was wearing goggles and a snug black hood attached to a matching coverall-like snowmobile suit. Paul could see no identifying marks. "Don't know. Let's not find out."

"What?" Howard hadn't heard him clearly. Before Paul spoke again, the snowmobile on the left turned in toward them as if to force their machine to turn away or stop—or tip over. "Goddam hot dog!" screamed Howard, and he spurted straight ahead, leaving the others behind. Paul almost fell off.

117

"What's with those bastards? Some kind of Hell's Angels on snow machines!" Howard complained.

"Can we shake 'em?" They were closing again on both sides.

"Probably," Howard slowed a little, "but it'll be damn dangerous. Can't see worth a shit." Their two pursuers pulled even. "Hang on!" With that, Howard's machine sprang forward. Paul gripped firmly and closed his eyes for a second. He heard the other motors drop behind, but then they were closer again—and seemed louder. He looked around. There were three! But just as they were pulling alongside in an apparent attempt to surround Howard's vehicle, they suddenly fanned outward. At that instant, Howard decelerated. Paul was thrown forward into his friend's back as their snowmobile plowed into and over a four-foot drift. The short flight ended with a jolting landing about eight inches to the left of a stalled taxi.

"My God!" Paul gasped, bumping against his companion.

"Fun, huh?" Howard grinned sideways and poked back an elbow. "They hemmed me in so I couldn't avoid it. Probably hoped we'd flip."

Paul managed a smile and nodded. "Here they come." The three black-and-green machines had rounded the drift and were speeding ahead to cut off their prey.

Howard circled sharply back to the left. "They actually did us a favor. Now I know how to get rid of them." He accelerated along the windward side of the growing drift and r-r-r-R-R-R-ROARED eastbound into 77th Street and a blinding gale of snow. "Here

118

goes," Howard bellowed. "We'll head into the Park. Bet I know it better than they do."

"What?" Paul couldn't hear him. He was trying hard not to be left behind.

By the time they reached Columbus Avenue, two of the other snowmobiles were again attempting to pull alongside. Ahead on the left slumbered the shadowy form of the American Museum of Natural History. The quartet of snow machines raced on toward Central Park, three abreast and one behind. Shaking snow from its fluffy face, a lost and shivering toy poodle looked up from its round nest in the snow and watched them disappear into the deluge of whiteness.

This time driving into the wind, Howard saw the headlights too late to turn. They were small, dim, and close-set: both nearsighted and cross-eyed. An old jeep on their left. Moving along mid-street, Howard's yellow-and-black machine passed so close to the squarish vehicle that Paul flinched away from its outside mirror. The snowmobile on the right had a clear path, but the one on the left met the jeep head on, rupturing the snow machine's gas tank. Its driver continued onward and upward through a billowing plume of orange and black till his forehead struck the top of the cab like a battering ram, and his flaming body flipped over onto the roof in a fatal inertial somersault that snapped his neck.

Knowing only that the left-hand machine had been stopped, Howard let out his boyhood battle cry, "W-e-ehawken!" as they leaned left and arched around to the north on Central Park West. One black-and-green snowmobile was close behind them on the right, but the other had fallen back, perhaps because of the mishap to the third. It soon reappeared, however, and the two pursuers once again pulled forward on both flanks. They seemed more determined than before. The one on the right pulled close and shouted, "Halt!" He was aiming a small black automatic.

"What do you think?" Howard asked over his shoulder.

"No! Don't believe 'em. Don't stop!"

Howard surged forward. There was a muffled report from the right rear. Then shouts: "Capture! No shots!"

The clouded image of the Hayden Planetarium drifted by on the left. Several dark shapes stood before the subway entrance at 81st Street. Overcoated police with flashlights probed the white wind for the motors they heard. But the trio of snow machines had turned away, into the wind—and into Central Park.

After nearly colliding with an abandoned car near the entrance to Transverse Road No. 2, Howard angled into a familiar but snow-clogged walkway. No stalled cars down here: only trees and benches. Almost immediately, he pulled off the path and sped into the white expanse of a buried field. Paul held on with rigid determination. He was tense and afraid. Frightened by the speed, by his inability to see, and by the unpredictable joltings and lurchings.

Howard was loose and limber, moving up and down in his crouch, leaning from side to side, guiding his machine around and over obstacles with skill and confidence. Paul was surprised and relieved by his friend's proficiency; this was not the sort of snowmobile ride he had anticipated. Howard must have had a lot more experience than he had realized. Paul tried to relax; he knew that it would be safer—and helpful to Howard. He was beginning to convince himself that the roller-coaster wouldn't fly off its track.

A smash from the side almost knocked them over. Turned-up skis hitting their hood. One of the black snowmobiles had rammed them, but not solidly. The two chasers were getting reckless, pressing from both sides. Howard angled to the right and entered an open grove of trees. He wove his way between dark trunks like a downhill skier racing the slalom. This forced the other snowmobilers to fall back into single file. But they too were skilled drivers and stayed close, the nearer one repeatedly bumping the yellow-and-black machine.

Paul's chin again pushed against Howard's back as they tilted uphill. Howard slowed slightly, as if teasing the others, then accelerated. Paul strained to see. Uphill, uphill, uphill. The crest! Howard cut power and veered—"Lean hard right!"—into a steep downhill chute. Their pursuers didn't anticipate the turn in time, and both black-and-green machines rolled out over the bluff and disappeared into the crystalline cascade.

At the bottom of the hill, Howard turned toward the east at a somewhat safer speed. Paul took a deep breath and touched his cheeks with a gloved hand. For the first time he noticed that his face was painfully cold. Howard looked back, grinning. "Let's cruise down Fifth Avenue."

Paul's watch showed 2:55 as he stepped onto the main deck of Coast Guard 138. The cutter was pitching slightly in choppy water at the mouth of the East River. Gusting wind flashed wave upon white wave of snow under a cluster of floodlights. Paul could barely make out the figure of Howard Tannenbaum watching on the pier below.

"You must be one important son of a bitch, Garfield," snapped the stubby, unsmiling Captain as he scrutinized Paul's identification cards. Then he looked up. "My name is Stort," and threw out his hand with the quickness of a fast draw.

Paul shook it. "I appreciate your efforts. I know these are unusual circumstances."

"I'll say they are. Unusual and goddam dangerous, I can tell you. Nobody in his right mind should be movin' in this miserable, rotten weather. It's gonna be rougher'n a cob, and we'll be all instruments till this storm quits." In spite of his brusque manner, Paul liked the feisty officer. He suspected that Captain Stort was not as displeased by the unexpected assignment as he let on, that he felt obliged to extract his pound of flesh in order to enjoy it.

The Captain looked at his watch. "We'll try to get you there in twelve hours—say, by fourteen hundred if we're lucky." His face twitched. "Now, I'll show you below. No fancy quarters, understand. This voyage wasn't exactly in my plans." Paul nodded in agreement.

12

WASHINGTON NATIONAL AIRPORT:
4:00 AM, FRIDAY, DECEMBER 22

TEMPERATURE: 25°F

BAROMETER: 29.11″ (FALLING)

WIND: NE 30–50 MPH

PRECIPITATION: HEAVY SNOW (24″)

FORECAST: SNOW ENDING THIS MORNING,
CLEARING AND COLD

"It's like an eye. Damn near calm." First Mate Atticus Morales was staring at an anemometer in the
chartroom of the U.S.S. *Narwhal*, one of several
oceanographic research vessels of the United States

Navy. "Strange—really strange." He looked up at Commander Claus Nansen, Captain of the *Narwhal*. "Ever been in a hurricane, sir?" As if to punctuate his query, a blast of wind jumped the needle to sixty knots. The quaking ship rose and plunged over the crest of a fifteen-foot wave, sending a storm of swirling papers into suspension from a desk where the Captain had been working. They floated and darted to all parts of the room.

"Yes, Morales, I *have* been in a hurricane." Commander Nansen steadied himself. "Many times. That was my job for four years. But never in December. This is the weirdest nor'easter I've ever seen." Then he stooped over and grasped a roll of graph paper. "Help me with this crap, will you?"

"Yes, sir." The First Mate had already picked up half a dozen papers.

"Four years," the Commander puffed. "I should say, twelve months' work and thirty-six months' waiting." He glanced at Morales from under gnarly white eyebrows. "I loved the storm-chasing but couldn't stand sitting around the rest of the time. Finally requested a transfer." He walked over to the map table and started squaring a handful of papers. "It was that background that got me drafted for this water-temperature project."

The ship rose and plunged again. The Captain braced himself and glanced at a radar screen. "You're right about this baby, Atticus. Damn winter storm is looking more and more like a giant tropical depression." He heaved a deep breath. "Wound up like a big, healthy hurricane is what it is. Where'd it get the extra heat to trigger this buildup? Craziest goddam thing I ever *heard* of! Way up north here against a cold front in the middle of December . . . and not *moving!*" He looked at the First Mate. "Reminds me of Hurricane Bella that stalled off Cuba."

As the *Narwhal* rolled level, Commander Nansen launched himself across the room. "The secret of survival in hurricanes is to *stay* inside the eye. The wind and waves wrapped around it'll knock you on your ass." He aimed his index finger at a button next to a speaker. "Horne," he bellowed, "can't you keep us inside this goddam thing?"

Static. *Squawk.* "I'm trying, sir. We should be quiet again in a minute. It's sure gettin' rough around the edges."

"Yes, we've noticed." The Captain turned away from the speaker. "Second time tonight we've drifted out. That was a hell of a blast we took before midnight."

"You've been up three watches in a row, Captain," observed Morales. "You'd better try to get some . . ." A redhaired civilian had appeared in the entranceway.

"Yes, McQuill?" Commander Nansen snapped, irritation showing on his face. "What now?" The Captain's abruptness was due to more than fatigue and concern about the storm. He resented the secretive "science types" on board over whom he had been given little real authority. And he resented not being informed about the details of their mysterious temperature-monitoring project.

McQuill's voice was tense. "We're ready to send the data for oh four hundred." He was tired of playing the Captain's game of having to ask permission for all transmissions. Most of them were in project code and would have been unintelligible to the Captain anyway.

The Captain lunged for his chair. "Any changes?"

"No, sir. Same story. Water temp's up another point five." McQuill was reading from a curled piece of paper perforated along two edges. "Surface pressure's down to two-eight point six-one."

"Holy Christ!" grunted Claus Nansen, clutching his desk. "We'll probably be stuck here through Christmas." Another unseen wave caused the ship to pitch and roll. After the three regained equilibrium, Nansen asked. "What about your equipment down below?"

"Still fouled up. Zero response." McQuill handed the Captain his paper. Nansen opened a drawer and picked a half-smoked cigar from the debris of his whalebone ashtray. Turning the butt in his mouth, he quickly reviewed the columns of typed digits. "Okay." He returned the paper. "And send Mr. Berger season's goddam greetings."

"Yes, sir," McQuill nodded. He stood there with his mouth open. He had other news the Captain hadn't heard yet.

The Commander looked up again. "Well?"

McQuill spoke excitedly. "Sonar just verified a large submarine at two hundred fathoms. It's in communication with the Soviet trawlers."

The western North Atlantic and eastern North America still lay in the earth's shadow. From 112 miles up, the cloud-coated night hemisphere seemed faintly phosphorescent in the reflected light of the three-quarter moon. A brightening fringe to the southeast marked the leading edge of dawn. The

126

growing storm below showed its eye as a small dark circle in the midst of an immense expanse of pale milk-white. Spots of gray around the center seemed strung together into streaks. They curved outward in great sweeping arms that revealed the counter-clockwise spin of a huge cyclonic spiral.

Like most artificial satellites designed for prolonged orbital operation, the Cosmos vehicle appeared strikingly awkward in full-deployment mode. A gigantic metallic insect. Panels of silicon cells spread from the ends of its articulated stalks, hungry for energy from the sun. Small red stars were painted on two sides of the central module, which shone silver in reflection against the black vacuum of space. Although seeming motionless, the Soviet robot was actually speeding southeastward relative to the turning earth. Its revolutionary velocity was slightly greater than the earth's rate of rotation, so that, like its five May Day sisters, the satellite passed over the same points on the planet's surface every twenty-four hours.

Through a transparent plate in its base, a cluster of cameras peered at the earth. And a thin beam of radiation reached downward with the ruby-red intensity of laser light.

Bzzzzzzt! Bzzzzzzt! The red light on the bedside telephone lit when the buzzer buzzed. *Bzzzzzzt! Bzzzzzzt!* At length, the First Lady poked her husband into consciousness with bony fingers. "Dear . . . dear. Wake up. It's your phone." The President was humped up like a dormant walrus. Suddenly he jerked upright and threw back the covers. "Yes, yes. I know, I know. Where the hell is it?" groping for the receiver. Then, "Yes? Hello? This is the President speaking."

"Mr. President, this is Herbert," came the reply. It was Herbert Salisbury, Special Assistant to the President. "I'm sorry to have awakened you, sir, but I'm afraid we have a very serious situation on our hands. I feel that I should brief you in person as soon as possible."

"Well, all right." The drowsy President slowly realized that Herbert sounded nervous. "Is it a military problem?" He hunched up into a sitting position against the headboard and yawned.

"No, not exactly. But it does require your immediate attention. May I meet you in your office in twenty minutes?"

"Uhh, twenty minutes? Very well." The President hung up and rubbed his eyes.

"What is it, dear?" The First Lady looked at him quizzically through half-closed eyes and tousled black hair.

"Damned if I know. Herb seems to think it's some sort of emergency. Supposed to meet him right away." The President swung around to sit on the edge of the bed and pushed his feet into wool-lined slippers. "Can you see the clock, Meg?"

"Yes, dear. It's four-twenty-one."

"Good morning, Mr. President." Herbert Salisbury was clutching a sheaf of papers. His high forehead wrinkled into a checkerboard of lines as he immediately began his report. "Two members of the National Security Council and one member of the Cabinet have requested that you convene an emergency meeting of the Council at the earliest

128

practicable time." Salisbury nodded his head for emphasis as he spoke. "That's why I thought I'd better wake you up and request this briefing." Wavy brown hair lay neatly molded to Herbert's narrow head. The ruddiness of his face accented his clear blue eyes.

The President strode across the Oval Office toward his desk and, with a wave of his hand, ushered his assistant to the red leather chair in front of it. "Be specific, Herb. Who and why?" The Chief Executive was of medium height and sturdy build. His penetrating brown eyes and square jaw were consistent with his reputation for keen perception and bluntness. Graying black hair fringed his balding head. He was wearing navy-blue slacks and a white shirt, sleeves folded back on his forearms.

"The Secretary of State, the Chairman of the Joint Chiefs of Staff, and the Secretary of Commerce." Salisbury laid some papers on the desk top and began unfolding a map. "The reason for the proposed meeting is to discuss the emergency created by the record-breaking storm that has paralyzed our northeast coast." He walked around behind the desk, presenting the map for the President's inspection. Pointing with his pen, "This snowstorm is approaching hurricane intensity and has not moved in almost twenty-four hours.

"It is unique in several of its characteristics." The President glanced up as Salisbury continued. "As you can see, it is affecting an abnormally large area, extending from way down here"—both leaned closer to the map—"south of Richmond, all the way to southern Maine. Snow depths and wind velocities have continued to increase throughout the night. Severe emergencies now exist in the entire storm area." Salisbury straightened up. "A growing body of opinion in the scientific community supports the conclusion that this storm is not entirely natural." Herbert sighed. His heavily furrowed brow and deep-set eyes gave him a particularly worried appearance.

The President rocked backward in his squeaking chair. He was flanked by the Presidential and American flags. "I'm not sure I understand, Herb. What does that mean, 'not entirely natural'?"

Salisbury started back around toward the front of the desk, looking at the Presidential Seal on the carpet as he spoke. "The Secretary of Commerce reports that a number of scientists in his Department—"

"Which agency?" asked the President.

Salisbury seated himself with a swish of air from the cushion. "NOAA, the National Oceanic and Atmospheric Administration. They include the National Weather Service."

"Go on."

"Well, many of our best-qualified meteorologists are apparently convinced that some sort of artificial weather modification must be involved in the fixation and intensification of this storm."

The President sat upright with a squeak. "Good God! Is that . . . ?" A man wearing a white steward's jacket knocked on the open door. "Come in, Edward," said the President. Then, turning to Salisbury, "I ordered coffee."

The man in the white jacket walked over to the desk and served them. He smiled hesitantly at Salisbury. "Cream, sir?"

"No, thank you, Edward." The steward promptly went out, closing the door behind him.

The President looked at Salisbury with an incredulous expression. "Damn, Herb, I didn't realize that such a thing was possible."

"Frankly, Mr. President, neither did I." Herbert picked up his cup and saucer. "But—and no one seems willing to commit himself without endless qualification—there is no doubt that the storm is behaving in an extraordinary way."

Salisbury stood up again and fingered a large "L" representing the center of low pressure on the map. "Of the greatest significance are these three facts." Counting on his fingers, "One, as I have mentioned already, the storm has stopped dead in its tracks." The President was sipping coffee, his eyes fixed on Salisbury. "Two, it has continued to intensify *in situ* since having become stalled. And three," Herbert's voice was rising, "people in the intelligence community have pointed out that the storm's center coincides almost exactly with the position of the so-called May Day intersection of Soviet satellites that caused so much concern last summer. Remember? When they concentrated all those ships beneath it?"

"Yes, certainly I remember, for God's sake. But I thought we concluded—everybody concluded—that the satellites were just for intelligence." The President put down his coffee cup and picked up a napkin.

"That is correct, sir. But that was before this blizzard developed." Salisbury began nervously pounding his right fist into his left hand. "The Secretary of State telephoned less than an hour ago—and he was in a very agitated state, if I may say so." The President stuck his little finger in his ear, which seemed to distract Herbert.

After a short pause, the President looked up. "Yes, go on."

"Intelligence reports have convinced the Secretary of the very definite possibility that the Soviets may have violated some of the articles of the SALT agreements which specifically prohibit weather-modification experiments that have potential for affecting other countries." He paused again as the President stood up. The Chief Executive raised his eyebrows, signaling him to continue. "Several Soviet vessels have again been detected in the storm area, including one large submarine. And—like last summer—there have been numerous transmissions between these ships and the Cosmos vehicles."

The President turned slowly toward the window, fingering his chin. Abruptly, "Let's meet at nine."

"I am glad to hear you say that, sir." Salisbury cleared his throat. "A lot of people are pooh-poohing this idea, but it's not one on which we can afford a miscalculation." The President compressed his lips and nodded. "I am afraid, however," Herbert continued, "that nine A.M. might be a little too soon. The extent to which air and ground travel have been immobilized is staggering. We had better allow extra time for the assembly of persons and materials." Salisbury clasped hands behind his back. "It seems to me that this will necessarily involve a considerable number and variety of participants and supporting documentation—especially if it gets to the point of initiating emergency measures."

"From the looks of that snow outside, Herb, I'd say emergency measures are a foregone conclusion."

"Yes, sir. I agree. On the state level, several Governors are already considering mobilization of National Guard units and are on the verge of requesting federal disaster relief." Herbert Salisbury was beginning to sound as though he enjoyed the emergency. He fairly trotted around the corner of the President's desk. "We shall have to arrange for transportation either underground via the emergency Metro access or by specialized snow vehicles—most of those would be military. As you can well imagine, there aren't many available around the District of Columbia. We ought to consider immediate conversion of the Metro to emergency status."

As was his habit, Herbert touched the President's forearm to emphasize a new point. "May I suggest noon rather than nine for the Council meeting? That would allow time for adequate preparations and for getting all of our people here."

"Good. That makes sense, Herb. We'd better cancel all morning appointments and move up my regular intelligence briefing to eight A.M. Will you get me the Metro plan?"

"Yes, sir," his assistant replied.

The President started toward the door, then turned. "And, Herb. No announcements, no press. Maximum security for now. This could be a bitch."

Sixteen minutes later, a phone rang in the darkened Pentagon office of Curtis Zimber. The Admiral nearly fell from the couch as he stretched and clamped his hand on the receiver. In a low voice he hoarsed, "Zimber."

"Popowski. Important news."

The Admiral urged his body into a sitting position. "Where are you?"

"Down the hall in my office. Secure line."

"All right, let's have it."

"Some of the weather-watchers are beginning to scream, and apparently they're getting through."

"What the hell does that mean?" The Admiral rose. "Spit it out." He was stroking his head with nervous motions. The fringing brown hair stuck out in all directions.

"A National Security Council meeting has been called for noon."

"Son of a bitch!" Zimber swung the receiver down against his thigh and sighed in frustration. Again speaking into the phone, "I thought we'd at least have today. What the hell time is it?"

"Five-fifteen."

"Shit." Zimber's black pupils were large in the semi-darkness. "Look, just make sure the Joint Chiefs and the Defense Secretary get the correct information. I'll get hold of Satin at CIA. We've got to buy time." He heaved another deep breath. "Who's here from project headquarters?"

"Panella. He's catching some sleep in the lounge. There's nothing new to report. Still no response, and the storm keeps getting worse."

"Have we got our rat in a cage?"

"Garfield? No, sir. Not yet."

"Not yet?" in a stage whisper. "Well, *when*?"

'That's problematical, Admiral. He got away from our security men on a snowmobile."

"Now isn't that cute. Goddammit, we've got to keep him quiet. Find him! I want Garfield on *ice!*"

13

~~~~~~

WASHINGTON NATIONAL AIRPORT:
   10:00 AM, FRIDAY, DECEMBER 22

TEMPERATURE: 24°F

BAROMETER: 28.93″ (FALLING)

WIND: NE 35–55 MPH

SNOW DEPTH: 2′10″ (DRIFTS TO 9′)

FORECAST: SNOW ENDING TODAY, CLEAR-
   ING AND COLDER TONIGHT

The Metro train began to accelerate just as Joni Dubin was sitting down. Pressed back against the seat, she heard her skis sliding backward on the floor. Almost immediately a voice announced, "Gallery Place,

Gallery Place." She wrapped herself in the arms of her blue parka and glanced around the car. It was nearly empty. Half a dozen men in Army uniforms and three civilians were forward; two other newcomers wearing wading boots were seated toward the rear. The emergency order must be preventing many stranded persons from using the subway, she thought, denying them the only safe means of transportation. But perhaps it was necessary.

Joni had been able to talk her way onto the train at the Rosslyn, Virginia, station because she had press credentials. Enforcement of the restrictions on Metro eligibility seemed to vary considerably. This was the first time the subway system had been placed on emergency status, and the multiplicity of rules and exceptions was not generally understood. Having changed lines at Metro Center, Joni was now on her way to Union Station–National Visitor Center, where she would exit. "Judiciary Square, Judiciary Square." She watched the dusky waffle walls of the huge tunnel flashing by.

Christopher Gonn's second call had been strange. If he could arrange for NASA people to meet Paul's ship, why hadn't he been able to get *her* transportation to the Washington Navy Yard as originally planned? He had seemed so sure the first time. But then, the entire affair was a puzzlement. Too bad the Greenbelt Road–Branch Avenue line wasn't open yet; she could have transferred and taken the Metro directly to the Navy Yard. Instead, she would try to ski there from Union Station. And she had thought that she was joking when she told Paul she might ski. Oh well, it's not very far, she reassured herself. Less than two miles.

Riding the Metro to Union Station was something Joni had done countless times, part of the regular routine of her life. This might have been the day before when she went to see David Bradford. Suddenly the familiar reality of the past—the sounds and motions of the train—put in perspective the seeming unreality of the present. Ski two miles through Washington? Joni realized that in a little more than twelve hours, she had somehow come to accept a truly bewildering series of events: the Conroy disappearance, Jane Conroy's telephone problems, Paul's mysterious mission, the unprecedented blizzard, Chris Gonn and NASA, the Coast Guard. Incredible!

One question led to another. What had happened to John Conroy? There was still no trace of him, and, as David Bradford had told her an hour before, there was little hope of finding any till after the storm. Why did Paul feel threatened? And by whom? Was he just making one of his old grandstand plays for attention? Substituting doing for giving as he had when they were married? No, that was hardly fair in these circumstances. But what in God's name was going on? She remembered that Paul had said not to trust anyone. What about Gonn? Maybe *his* phone is tapped. Maybe *mine* is! Joni was becoming uneasy. "Union Station–National Visitor Center," from the speaker. "Union Station–National Visitor Center."

Joni's eyes again focused on the interior of the car. She looked at her watch; it was 10:55. Grasping a railing, she stood up and retrieved her ski equipment, then walked to the sliding doors. Her ski boots felt large and clumsy: ka-lump, ka-lump. When the train glided to a halt, she stepped awkwardly onto the platform, skis under one arm, poles in the other.

The subway terminal in the west wing of the renovated Union Station building was abnormally congested. And hundreds of people—perhaps several thousand—crowded the adjoining Hall of States and Main Hall of the National Visitor Center. They were refugees from the storm. Some were stranded by unstarting trains; others were simply taking shelter. How many outside hadn't found refuge?

Joni studied the scene in amazement. It reminded her of a wartime movie. Soldiers were standing around in groups, talking excitedly, waiting for something to do; Red Cross workers were wrapping blankets around people lying on the floor; Park Service employees were distributing hot food and beverages. In the center of the Main Hall, a captive audience lined tiered galleries above the open theater, where an ever-changing mosaic of color slides entitled "Welcome to Washington" played across eighty screens.

Joni started toward the station doors, holding her skis and poles vertically against her body. Several soldiers in a nearby cluster noticed her and turned to show off. Despite the presence of federal military personnel, and rumors of impending martial law, National Park Service and District of Columbia police were still in charge of law enforcement. A line of overcoated officers protected the front exits.

"Yes, ma'am. Where do you think you're goin'?"

"Outside."

"Goin' skiing?" laughed a second policeman.

"Yes, but not for pleasure." She smiled in her charming way. "I know it may seem crazy, but I do have to get someplace out there, so . . ." Sort of waving the skis in the air, "I figured this would be the only way of doing it."

"You serious?"

"Yes I am, officer. I'm a member of the press, and it's extremely important." The short, curly-haired policeman on the right whispered something to his neighbor, and both broke into sputtering guffaws.

"May I see some identification?" asked the first officer, who had not joined in the joke.

Joni unzipped her parka and produced a folder full of cards. "They let me on the Metro as a representative of the press," she explained, hoping for similar cooperation.

The policeman glanced at her credentials and started nodding knowingly. "Yeah, sure. You did look familiar. I guess it pays to be well known, huh?" He thrust the cards back toward her. "But I can't let you go out there." He smiled. "I'd never get to see you on the tube again."

She decided not to try to explain her reasons. Instead, smiling warmly, "It's really not as bad as you think. You must be a Southerner. I've seen worse than this lots of times in the Rocky Mountains."

"Worse than this, huh? You don't—"

"Well, at least as bad," not giving him a chance. "Believe me, I can handle it. And it is very, *very* important to me." Joni touched his glove. "I'll be all right."

"I hope so." He yielded. "Please be careful, Miss Dubin." She stopped in the space between the doors to put on her short cross-country skis.

The wind was moaning as she pushed out into the blizzard. Immediately she had to traverse a streaming five-foot drift. Joni loved skiing. It would be fun now if it weren't for poor visibility and constant buffeting by the wind. She caught a glimpse of two men rushing out of the station behind her. They looked like the same pair that had sat in the rear of her train car. Wonder what *they* told the guards? Above them, over the left-hand arch of the main building, Joni noticed a bold inscription chiseled in white marble. She could barely read it through the blowing snow:

FIRE • GREATEST OF DISCOVERIES
ENABLING MAN TO LIVE IN VARIOUS
CLIMATES USE MANY FOODS • AND COMPEL
THE FORCES OF NATURE TO DO HIS WORK

Turning away, she poled around the frozen mound that was Columbus Fountain and aimed southwestward into Delaware Avenue. To her relief, this put the wind at her back. It had already sucked the indoor warmth from her face. She glanced up. There was no definite sky; the milky blur just looked darker overhead. All light seemed to emanate from the snow below. A cold white incandescence. Joni felt exhilarated now. Hers was a challenge beyond ordinary experience, a magnificent adventure. She propelled herself onward, genuinely thrilled in what she perceived to be a heroic undertaking.

On the left rose the Russell Senate Office Building. One block over was the Dirksen Building and David Bradford's office. When she had left it twenty-four hours before, the sidewalks and streets had still been dry. Now some snowdrifts were ten feet deep.

As she swerved to skirt a large drift, Joni saw two dark shapes from the corner of her eye. She turned to look. The men were close behind her, struggling through the snow with great difficulty. They must be going to the Capitol. But why not underground, she wondered. Maybe they're reporters. She crossed Constitution Avenue and entered the Capitol

140

grounds, turning into the roadway that passed directly in back of the great edifice. A recently plowed path made travel easier, but gale winds were quickly filling in the gaps that had been cut through the drifts. She glanced at the Capitol. Its dome was obscured in whiteness.

The two men did not turn toward the building but continued following Joni. They were trotting rapidly through the shallower snow of the cleared lane and gaining on her. Chasing her! Her heart bolted. Muggers? Rapists? She hesitated, then poled frantically as they broke into a lunging run. She kept a few feet in front, helped by the wind. One slip and they would have her. The leader tried to step on the ends of her skis, then stretched forward to grab her. She twisted and thrust her right pole as a warning. It struck him in the face and came back bloody.

Strengthened by terror, she angled left and raced out of the Capitol grounds. The two men had stopped. Abruptly she was slowed almost to a halt crossing snow-clogged Independence Avenue. She shoved herself into New Jersey Avenue between the House office buildings. The street was buried by snow. She looked behind. One of the men was coming again and closing fast.

She had to weave back and forth around six-foot drifts, searching for low places. Her pursuer attempted a straighter course. He lunged and hurled himself over the snow, falling and crawling. But his efforts were futile in the deep white morass. Joni pulled steadily ahead and left him wallowing hopelessly in the drifts.

The blizzard was screaming out of the northeast, tearing at her from the left rear. Again unshielded by buildings, she had trouble maintaining her balance. Snow grains felt abrasive as they grazed the skin of her cheek. The cold penetrated her clothing and chilled her body. Her toes were numb. Slowly this cross-country adventure was transforming into agony. She began to consider that she might not be able to make it. She shouldn't have tried on skis. The Washington Navy Yard seemed impossibly far.

14

~~~~~~

NEW LONDON NAVAL SUBMARINE BASE:
11:00 AM, FRIDAY, DECEMBER 22

TEMPERATURE: 22°F

BAROMETER: 29.07 " (FALLING)

WIND: SE 25–50 MPH

SNOW DEPTH: 3' (DRIFTS TO 10')

FORECAST: SNOW ENDING TODAY,
CLEARING AND COLDER TONIGHT

"I don't believe it. We're finally movin'." Matthew
Rodek turned away from the porthole and eyed
Duncan Smith. "We shoulda shoved off four hours
ago. If you're gonna have an emergency plan, then

you damn sure oughta be ready ta go on a moment's notice. Sloppy planning." His companion was sitting on the far side of the table in the officers' saloon of the U.S.S. *Manatee.* "I never shoulda got up yesterday," Rodek went on. "Things have been behind schedule and screwed up ever since." He jerked out a chair and flopped down into it.

"I guess a lot of people have had to change plans," the other offered unsympathetically. Lieutenant Commander Duncan Smith was a bright, conscientious young officer. Textbook Annapolis. Six feet, 180 pounds, neatly parted brown hair, serious sea-green eyes. And his uniform was immaculate. Typical new breed, in Rodek's view. Matthew Rodek had enlisted and drawn hazardous-duty pay in submarines before Smith was born. The two had little in common; they tolerated each other out of necessity. Rodek had broken Smith in as his successor in piloting *Nessie,* the Navy's abyssal bathyscaphe. "We may still be home in time for Christmas," Smith suggested.

"Don't bet on it." Rodek slouched back and clasped hands behind his head. "Not the way things are goin'."

"Were you planning to spend the holidays with family?"

"Me and my brother were s'posed to fly to Vegas this afternoon." Matthew glanced at the bulkhead clock: 11:35.

"You were never married, were you?" Smith inquired.

"Nope." Rodek frowned. "Not a chance. Got better things to do—like workin' the Strip in Big V."

Smith leaned forward. "Look, you didn't *have* to come back for this mission."

144

"Yes I did. But not for the same reason as you. You're under orders. I'm here for my New Year's stake." Rodek pulled a deck of cards from his shirt pocket and started shuffling. "Play a little gin?"

"No thanks." Smith was rotating a pencil. "I meant that I don't understand why they interrupted your schedule. I'm fully capable of taking *Nessie* down myself."

"Sure you are." Matthew was dealing draw poker to himself and two imaginary players. "But your job on this run is that goddam bomb. Anyway, something big like this needs a backup pilot."

"Do you think there's much chance of trouble?"

"Hell yes." Rodek examined his tight hand cautiously as though the other players were real and might sneak a look. "First problem is to get close enough to drop. The swells are gonna be murder."

"I was thinking about the Soviets."

"Ahh, don't believe that bullshit. Makes no sense that we're after the Russians on this."

"Who then?" Smith sat up straighter.

"Never tip your hand." Matthew grinned. He held four spades, so he drew one card. The pack on the table was slowly spreading out as the *Manatee* began to feel the five-foot waves in Fishers Island Sound.

Duncan Smith sighed in annoyance. Abruptly he stood up and walked to a porthole. His view was of a horizontal torrent of white.

After nine hours on the wildly heaving CG 138, Paul Garfield had nothing left to throw up. He lay curled in his bunk, trying to transport his mind to peaceful places. It was his dentist-office stratagem, one that had always helped ease pain and anxiety under

145

the high-speed drill. Already on this endless turbulent voyage, he had thought many times of the mountains. Of clear alpine dawns, warm midday meadows, and cool afternoon shadows under virgin spruce. He had thought of skiing. Weaving downslope through pure, fresh powder. And lying afterward in the light of a fire. Of making love. Joni. Their erstwhile gentle joy.

He concentrated on these scenes and others, over and over. A rolling kaleidoscope of recall. Anything to help his gut forget its craving to retch. He went fishing. Wading a rippling summer trout stream, canoeing a still forest lake, diving to the exotic beauty of a coral reef. And trolling the Gulf Stream for . . . ohhh, a bad choice. He groaned. Rarely on the ocean had he avoided the devil of vomit. Only on smooth water. He had a landlubber's stomach. *Oh,* for smooth water. Smooth, calm water.

This chaotic trip couldn't last much longer. They must be nearing Cape Charles. If only he had understood sooner, grasped the significance of Conroy's resignation and disappearance. He could have flown to Washington with Jane. He should have gone with her anyway—for her peace of mind. She had undoubtedly hoped that he would. And now Zimber was after *him.* Even though miserably seasick, at least he felt safe with the Coast Guard. He doubted that the Admiral would risk involving them in his machinations. But the Washington Navy Yard—that could be trouble.

Would Chris Gonn and Joni be there to meet him? Hell, if Chris could get a Coast Guard cutter, he certainly should be able to arrange for protection and transportation. Snow vehicles of some kind. And Joni would be there, he was sure of that. She was unfailingly resourceful, had always kept her commitments. Unlike himself. He clutched his pillow and wrapped around it in the fetal position.

The ship rose and plunged, rose and plunged. Paul had concluded that the quickest and most effective way of delivering his information and accomplishing his mission in Washington would be through David Bradford. The Senator's subcommittee had been probing unauthorized military projects, and Bradford was already eager to interview Paul. Most important at this point, Senator Bradford was in a position to circumvent the Pentagon and gain immediate access to the White House.

Paul turned to face the bulkhead, still hugging his pillow. The ship churned onward. It was ironic but perhaps just that he should go to Bradford to try to undo the misguided past. Warm, selfless Bradford to whom Joni had so often compared Paul unfavorably. For a number of years, Paul had blamed him for Joni's alienation and decision to get a divorce.

Bradford had been a popular, glamorous figure. An Olympic hero fighting the political establishment. His cause had been something in which Joni could immerse herself totally: emotionally, intellectually, and physically. It stood in sharp contrast to Paul's monastic existence as an astrophysicist. When Paul had met Joni in Boulder during their first year of graduate school at the University of Colorado, they seemed to have everything in common. They went everywhere and did everything together. Their young love permeated the fabric of their lives. But not long after their marriage, Paul had found himself converted to the religion of science; he became an in-

147

creasingly devout monk in the rigorous brotherhood of research.

Later, when he had been elevated to postdoctoral priesthood at the National Center for Atmospheric Research in Boulder, their paths diverged even more. Joni worked for a television station in Denver and was active in politics. And she and David Bradford had fallen in love. "I can't give to someone as completely wrapped up in himself as you are," she had told Paul. "I need something in return." It was over.

Bradford had not been without hypocrisy and self-interest, Paul reminded himself. When David decided to run for Congress, he and Joni broke off their covert affair, and Bradford married Carla, his high-school sweetheart. A mixed marriage would've been a political liability. If that wasn't a case of ambition over love, what was? But Joni had bought it. She sacrificed her feelings to Bradford's future. She thought that he could be the first Black President. Maybe he could. His career was well on its way.

There were many coincidences and ironies, Paul mused. All three of them had moved to Washington, D.C.—well, Joni's move there probably hadn't been as coincidental as Paul's. And now uncontrolled events were bringing Paul and Joni together, providing an opportunity he had longed for. Perhaps, after the present business was over, there would be another chance for them. The circumstances of the storm would force him to confess errors of judgment in his career; they might also be a means of washing away the mistakes of their marriage, purging the past. Breaking clouds could symbolize a new beginning.

CG 138 lifted over an enormous wave and slammed down with jarring impact. Paul braced himself to keep from falling from his bunk. He moaned and turned over. New spasms of nausea had begun, and they wouldn't stop. He drew long, deep breaths. He was in a state of torture. He would gladly have told anyone anything he knew simply to end his ordeal. Ordeal by motion. There was no relief, no escape. Only waiting and thinking.

Torture. The old cliché: Everyone has his breaking point. Torture could be deemed successful, he supposed, if it squeezed one past that point. A mild threat might work for one, but not even death for another. Paul was sure that he would be easy. Oh, yes. Oh, yes. Oh, yes.

How can torture hold any fascination for people? Something lurks there, perhaps in everyone. More than simple curiosity. Something sadistic. A desire to be horrified? Maybe that's it: reinforcement of self-righteousness through disgust.

"You don't look very healthy to me, I can tell you." Captain Stort was looking through the cabin doorway. He offered his most worried facial expression. "But we'll be in the Bay before long, Garfield. Won't be so bad then." He staggered in. "Worst goddam storm I've ever seen." The Captain grunted. "I hope there's somebody to pick you up. Our word is they've got three feet of snow with heavy drifting. Worst miserable blizzard on record." He leaned over the bunk and patted Paul's leg. "Should put in about fourteen hundred hours. Hang on there, mister." Paul simply rocked back and forth, slowly and steadily. Like the ship.

149

* * *

"My God, Dubin! You must've been outa your goddam gourd to try a stunt like that." Ralph Kirkpatrick rolled forward in the squealing chair and
reached for his pipe. The sign on his desk said CITY
EDITOR. "You're lucky you found your way over here.
By rights, you oughta be up to your ass in a snowbank." Joni's ill-shaven friend scraped a wooden
match across the sole of his shoe and started puffing
on his pipe.

"Well, up until the last minute I expected to have
a ride," she explained. "And I had no idea how incredibly bad it would be." Although still unnerved
and confused by the bizarre chase behind the Capitol,
Joni had determined not to tell Kirkpatrick about it.
Unsure of his reaction, she didn't want to complicate
her already improbable story. Her inquisitive colleague might be disinclined to help her without a full
explanation of what she was doing. "By the time I
crossed the railroad tracks, I was completely exhausted. Thank God I thought of you and found somebody here." Joni's parka was unzipped with the hood
down. She began unsnarling her hair with a pale-blue
comb. Her warming cheeks were bright crimson.

"You kiddin'? *The Star-News* never closes." He
smiled broadly. Ralph Kirkpatrick was a longshore-
man disguised as Teddy Roosevelt. Large, powerful,
and outspoken, he had a ruddy, mustached face with
round glasses and short, wavy hair. Aromatic smoke
curled up from his briar bowl. "Hell, I never did get
home last night. I kept stallin' as the storm got worse,
waitin' for it to let up. Lot of people got stuck here.
Hell of it is, we can't get out any papers. Five'll
getcha ten our trucks won't move for two or three

150

days now. Some goddam Christmas present," he muttered.

"I was surprised to find the place so busy," noted Joni.

"Christ, yes. We're goin' crazy. Storm news pilin' up, and everybody outside the blizzard wants to know what's goin' on. All we can do is feed stuff to the wires. Phone circuits are mostly jammed; some have quit. There's your irony: We've got the makin's of a major natural disaster on our hands, and the whole goddam world can read about it but us!" He waved to someone walking past the front of his office, then turned back to his visitor. "Why in *hell* do you want to go to the Navy Yard?"

"I'm sorry, Kirk. I can't tell you now. But it *is* urgent."

"So you said, but I can't imagine what could be goin' on in that goddam place—especially during this blizzard." He reached for his phone. "Our outdoor editor turned up this morning with his snowmobile. . . . Oh, Lois, ring Mr. Mennis' desk for me, please." Glancing up at Joni, "He'll be tickled to run you down there. Loves to show off. . . . Hello, Red? . . . Yeah. Say, listen, old buddy, I've got a good friend here who needs a little outdoor help. Can ya stop by for a minute? . . . Good. Thanks." Clank. "He'll be right here."

"Thank you, Kirk." She smiled gently, sincerely.

"Sure. I'll get a chance to cash in the favor. Say, have you gotten wind of a National Security Council meeting?"

"Today?" Joni wondered.

"Yeah." He eyed the clock. "Right now. Noon."

151

"No, but I haven't talked to anyone. I gather you have."

"Uh-huh. All kinds of rumors. A couple of our boys are tryin' to tell me the Ruskis pumped up this storm."

15

~~~~~~

WASHINGTON NATIONAL AIRPORT:
NOON, FRIDAY, DECEMBER 22

TEMPERATURE: 24°F

BAROMETER: 28.87″ (FALLING)

WIND: NE 35–60 MPH

SNOW DEPTH: 3′2″ (DRIFTS TO 11′)

FORECAST: SNOW ENDING TODAY, CLEAR-
ING AND COLDER TONIGHT

Thomas Jefferson and Andrew Jackson overlooked
the proceedings. So did Daniel Webster. Thirteen
persons were seated around the long elliptical table
in the Cabinet Room of the White House. At its head

stood the President of the United States. Seated on his immediate right was the Vice President. An emergency meeting of the National Security Council had just begun.

Statements read by André Geler, Director of the National Oceanic and Atmospheric Administration, and Vincent Satin, Director of the Central Intelligence Agency, had established the seriousness of the crisis. Silent shock was the mood of the room. The President began speaking. "I thank Dr. Geler and Director Satin for their informative reports." The Chief Executive was wearing a gray business suit. His expression was stern, his voice tense. "It now seems clear that a very dangerous situation confronts us.

"We had all hoped that the blizzard would abate before the start of this meeting. Instead," the President went on, "we learn that it has continued to worsen and is now of unprecedented size and severity. I am afraid that the coincidence of Soviet activity with the center of this stationary storm—as just convincingly documented by Mr. Satin—brings us to the brink of a grave international crisis."

General Walter Wilcox, Chairman of the Joint Chiefs of Staff, was seated on the President's left near the middle of the table. He abruptly shoved back his chair to attract attention. "General Wilcox?" His Commander in Chief yielded the floor.

"Mr. President." The massive General rose to his feet, jerking downward on his jacket of Air Force blue. "I for one think that we are already *over* the brink." He cleared his throat noisily. "It is my conviction that the combination of the two compelling lines of evidence here presented is conclusive."

He cleared his throat again and proceeded in his characteristically wordy fashion.

"There certainly can be no reasonable doubt about the fact that we are suffering the ravages of an extraordinary meteorological phenomenon. Far too extraordinary in its intensity and immobility to be explained any longer as a simple freak of nature." As he was speaking, a young lady in a blue pants suit entered the room and handed a piece of paper to Secretary of Defense Lloyd Norris.

"And now we have been shown," General Wilcox continued, "that the center of this abnormal storm underlies with uncanny mathematical exactitude the orbital intersection of the so-called May Day satellites of the Soviet Union *and* coincides with the site of last summer's unusual concentration of Soviet ships." The Chairman of the Joint Chiefs was expounding mechanically, as though his remarks had been rehearsed. He rotated his large head slowly to scan all faces around the table.

"Moreover, the presence of three Soviet trawlers and one of their new nuclear submarines in the storm area has been reconfirmed this very morning. So has a continuation of radio transmissions between these ships and the superjacent satellites. There is simply no question about it. The evidence is conclusive," he repeated. The gray-haired General was determined to establish his point of view early in the meeting. "And this conclusion is reinforced by reports which we have been receiving throughout the past twelve hours from military intelligence sources."

"What *is* the conclusion, Walter?" queried the President impatiently, arms folded across his chest.

"That the Russians are experimenting with weather warfare!"

"Nonsense," muttered the Secretary of State.

"Excuse me, Mr. President," interrupted Secretary of Defense Norris, who was sitting across from General Wilcox. He spoke slowly in a deep resonant voice with a trace of Southern accent. "I have just been informed that one of the Navy's research vessels has detected a second Soviet submarine beneath the storm center."

General Wilcox turned up his palms. "There you have it! Now, I want to underline not only my confidence in the accuracy and reliability of our intelligence but, *more* important, my conviction that decisive action is in order. Indeed, I consider decisive action to be *imperative*." The frowning Chairman remained standing.

"Do you have specific recommendations, General?" persisted the President.

On the General's right, the Director of the CIA leaned forward in his chair. "Mr. President, I concur with the opinion of General Wilcox, and I would like to offer a recommendation myself." Director Satin's glossy black hair was combed straight back over his head. His normal facial expression was a sort of caustic smirk, so that one expected him to say something sarcastic.

"Go ahead, Vincent." The President nodded. He was conducting this meeting in his customary manner, listening to the opinions of his colleagues with little comment of his own. They in turn, had formed the habit of addressing themselves primarily to the Chief Executive. When he had reached a decision, he would make it known.

Director Satin proceeded. "I recommend that the National Military Command Center in the Pentagon be instructed to place the armed forces of the United States on immediate worldwide stand-by alert." Satin's thin dark eyebrows drew down into a V behind his gold-framed bifocals.

"Good!" snapped the Chairman of the Joint Chiefs. He sat down. A murmur of mingled conversations spread throughout the room.

First to object to Satin's proposal was Wilson Keithley-Smythe, the President's somber National Security Advisor. He was sitting on the Chief Executive's immediate left, next to Vincent Satin. He said simply, "I think that would be unwise at this point."

Secretary of State Charles Kroner, seated between the Vice President and the Secretary of Defense, promptly expanded Keithley-Smythe's thesis. "Given the present situation, I believe that a move such as that recommended by Director Satin would be premature and unnecessarily provocative, especially prior to an informal inquiry of the Soviet Union at the very least." The lanky New Englander's gray crewcut seemed to bristle. He pulled off his horn-rimmed glasses and glared at General Wilcox.

"Our evidence is circumstantial and is *not* conclusive beyond reasonable doubt. I agree that there are grounds for suspicion. Perhaps there has been a violation of SALT prohibitions against weather modification. But let us not stampede into careless decisions. We should proceed with caution and hear what the Soviets have to say before considering *any* action."

"Bullshit!" barked General Wilcox with a toss of his hand. "That's all we'll get from them. They've

157

lied about this operation from the start. We let them get away with it last summer when I recommended a firmer stand, and now look what we've got. This is a goddam emergency, Kroner!" He lowered his voice. "Besides, Vince only proposed stand-by. Personally I think we should go on *full* alert."

"A little muscle," added Secretary of Defense Norris, "*could* serve to underscore the seriousness of any inquiry or protest as proposed by Secretary Kroner." The balding Defense Secretary returned his ever-present pipe to his mouth.

The Deputy Secretary of Defense, seated on Norris's right, waved his hand for attention. "May I offer a suggestion?"

"Mr. Muehlenbachs?" the President recognized him. The young blond administrator stood up.

"Mr. President, this seems to me to be an appropriate time to use the Hot Line. Tell the Soviet Chairman why we're going on alert and demand immediate cessation of all their activities in the storm area."

"He'll just say they're studying the weather," carped General Wilcox.

"Karl's absolutely right." Secretary Norris supported his Deputy. His voice was more forceful than before. "This situation has become a major disaster literally overnight. Hundreds of American citizens are dying. But we can't do much to help those affected until the storm is stopped. We must have immediate results. Tell the Russians to shut it off or risk retaliation!"

The Vice President asked for recognition and rose to her feet. Elizabeth Lindemann was a handsome woman in her early fifties. The petite lady from

Texas had short black hair and a reserved, businesslike presence. She rarely spoke at these meetings, but her colleagues had learned to listen when she did. They afforded her full attention.

"Mr. President, I strongly disagree with the contentious opinions which have just been expressed. Although the emergency we face is both unexpected and extreme, precipitous decisions have no less potential for destruction. We can ill afford to make matters worse. Overreaction and ultimata cannot be justified by what amounts to little more than a collection of unfounded allegations." The Vice President paused for a moment, then seated herself.

The President was nodding. "Well said, Elizabeth. I agree." He had heard enough discussion. He turned to Keithley-Smythe. "We will make an informal inquiry of the Soviet Union before considering further action." The murmuring began again. "Contact Ambassador Smekov as soon as possible."

"Of course, Mr. President."

"Emphasize our need for an immediate explanation of their activities and intentions." Keithley-Smythe rose and hurried from the room. Secretary of State Kroner sighed in relief and glanced at the clock behind the President. It was 12:49.

"Either the Russians aren't responsible for this storm, or they neglected to inform their Embassy," commented the Director of the CIA in a futile attempt to lighten the atmosphere. "Their whole staff is snowbound just like everybody else."

General Wilcox again pushed up from his chair. "Mr. President, as a precautionary step pending response from the Soviets, I strongly urge that we start a fleet of destroyers and attack submarines on their

159

way to the locality in question. We may need them in a hurry later on."

"The man makes sense, Mr. President," agreed Defense Secretary Norris.

"Perhaps. Get me tactical specifics," requested the Commander in Chief.

"Yes, sir." And General Wilcox marched toward the door.

During the remainder of the meeting, the Council concentrated on two critical areas: national security and disaster relief. First came decisions regarding the maintenance of all military and governmental functions that are essential to full emergency preparedness, primarily transportation and communication. Then, following a brief discussion, the Chief Executive decided not to declare a national emergency. However, there was general agreement that he should immediately designate the entire northeast coast a National Disaster Area, making parts of eleven states eligible for federal assistance.

So that the Council could appreciate the full impact of the disaster and focus attention on the most serious domestic problems, a series of invited reports was presented by experts representing the areas of major concern. The Mayor of Washington, D.C., described the situation in the national capital itself, but freely admitted that conditions were probably as bad or worse in other metropolitan areas within the blizzard zone.

The Mayor's voice was full of anxiety. "No traffic is moving in the District of Columbia except Metro trains belowground and specialized vehicles aboveground—that is, tread-traction machines such as snowmobiles, bulldozers, tanks, and snow cats. And may I say here, Mr. President," glancing at the Chief Executive, "my office has been deluged by complaints protesting your restriction of access to the Metro system. I know that MATA"—the Washington Metropolitan Area Transit Authority—"is getting the same reaction."

"Snow removal," the Mayor confessed, "is almost totally ineffective here because we have virtually no equipment. But even out at Dulles Airport, where they are well equipped, it's a hopeless task against these gale winds and the heavy snow. I suggest that all military and government vehicles capable of operating in deep snow be mobilized immediately."

Problems of communication were summarized by Chairman Morris Persoff of the Federal Communications Commission. "Of course, wires and cables are blowing down and cannot be repaired under present conditions. Other interruptions are apparently being caused by freeze-thaw effects and flooding, due to both melting snow and high surf along waterfronts. Mr. Salisbury tells me that a few leaks have even been reported in the White House." The Chairman chuckled a little. Herbert Salisbury's brow pulled down into a frown. He was sitting on the far right-hand side of the table between Deputy Defense Secretary Muehlenbachs and the President's science advisor, Dr. Albert Kaufman.

"Telephone circuits," Chairman Persoff explained, "are almost continually tied up by calls in and out of the snow zone as the rest of the country tries to find out what's happening. The Commission recommends that telephone service be restricted to official use for the duration of this emergency.

"The electronic media remain government's most

161

effective means of communication. Incidentally, most radio and television stations either have suspended or are prepared to suspend normal programming. As in just about every other industry and activity, most of their personnel have been stuck at work overnight or prevented from leaving home this morning."

The Director of the Federal Disaster Assistance Administration, Malcom White, was visibly disconcerted by the enormity of the problems he faced. He gave a disturbing account of the hardships wrought on individual citizens by the storm. "Shortages of fuel for heating and power generation—and the failure of utility services in general—constitute a growing but not yet critical menace. The paralysis of transportation, however, has stranded literally millions of persons away from their homes, most of them without food or medical supplies.

"The more fortunate are in their places of employment or in public facilities." Mr. White's voice cracked with emotion. "God knows how many failed to reach or remain inside adequate shelter. Estimates of storm-related deaths now exceed one thousand, but these are tentative and undoubtedly conservative guesses." He sighed heavily.

"Organized looting has been reported in many cities, including the Washington area. We did expect that; it happened in Buffalo, New York, when it was snowbound during the winter of '77.

"At sea, of course, all unauthorized ships and planes have been ordered out of the storm area. Unfortunately, the warnings came too late for some. I was told just prior to this meeting that a Liberian freighter is breaking up off Cape Hatteras and an Italian passenger liner may be in serious trouble."

At the conclusion of these reports, the National Security Council adopted a preliminary plan to facilitate the provision of basic needs to the populace of the blizzard zone: transportation and snow removal, shelter and utilities, food and medical supplies, communication. Central to this proposal was the recommendation that an *ad hoc* Blizzard Relief Council be created to oversee disaster relief and recovery. A draft-outline was to be presented for consideration by the Domestic Council at its emergency meeting scheduled for 2:00 P.M. It was obvious to all, however, that the effectiveness of any plan would be minimal until the weather improved.

The President wiped his forehead with a handkerchief and began his concluding remarks. "I know that we are all beginning to feel the strain of this unprecedented national crisis. Those of us due to meet with the Domestic Council in less than one hour will soon feel it even more. However, I trust that you now understand clearly the need for all of us to remain immediately available. And—as I announced at the outset—the importance of our next meeting this evening, which for all practical purposes will be a continuation of the current session.

"Unless I hear serious objection, I intend to invite the bipartisan Congressional leadership to that meeting. I shall brief them personally later this afternoon." The President put his hands on his hips and looked around the large table. Vincent Satin shifted his position in his chair and appeared ready to speak. But he said nothing, intimidated by the President's uncompromising tone. There was no objection. "*And* I shall invite the leadership to all subsequent meetings which we may deem necessary during this crisis." Gazing down at the papers before him, he added, "It is indicative of the suddenness and magnitude of the emergency that some of those whom we invite here may be physically unable to join us."

The President looked up again. "Now, let me remind you of the necessity of maintaining security. Until further notice, *all* press releases relevant to our deliberations will be made in the White House Press Room subject to my prior approval. No exceptions." He paused and took a deep breath.

"Tonight we shall evaluate the Soviet reply to our inquiry—unless events dictate more immediate action—and we shall hear updated testimony as to the causes and effects of this storm. Bear in mind the real possibility of having to make potentially dangerous tactical decisions. God willing, the storm will have ended by then.

"As you know, emergency quarters are being arranged for you in the Old Executive Office Building across the street, accessible underground from the White House." The President nodded toward the draperied, high-arched windows. "Somehow the name 'White House' has never seemed more appropriate. Well, I now adjourn this meeting until eight o'clock this evening." It was 1:21 P.M.

Dan Simon, White House Press Secretary, immediately called the President aside. "Mr. President, the reporters are driving me up the wall. The Press Room is jammed. The word is out on this meeting— no way to keep it secret—plus a number of them are trying to make a connection between the storm and the May Day satellite incident. The arrival of soldiers in the city has triggered all sorts of rumors: martial law, international crisis. Sir, we've got to issue some sort of statement."

"All right, Dan. But not one word even *implying* that there is anything unnatural about the storm *or* that we are contacting the Russians. The last thing we need is to feed public panic. Make your statement brief and strictly disaster-relief. Announce the National Disaster designation, the Domestic Council meeting, and the proposed formation of a Blizzard Relief Council. Hell, recite the weather report: 'Snow ending today, clearing and colder tonight.' Let us pray that the forecast is accurate." Over Mr. Simon's shoulder, the President saw General Wilcox rushing into the room with a handful of papers. "Oh dear. Here come the battle plans."

16

~~~~~~

WASHINGTON NATIONAL AIRPORT:
1:00 PM, FRIDAY, DECEMBER 22

TEMPERATURE: 24°F

BAROMETER: 28.84″ (FALLING)

WIND: NE 35–60 MPH

SNOW DEPTH: 3′4″ (DRIFTS TO 12′)

FORECAST: SNOW ENDING TODAY, CLEAR-
ING AND COLDER TONIGHT

Joni Dubin peered out through the window of the Navy Yard dock house. She knew that the pier and the Anacostia River were just fifty feet in front of her, but she couldn't see them. The howling white

166

wind allowed vision to reach only a few yards. She looked at her watch: 1:25.

She and Red had had an easier time getting there than she had expected, thanks to an enormous bulldozer that was operating continually along the quarter-mile driveway. The guard at the gate had recognized Red, and they had talked about guns. Joni smiled to herself: Red had introduced her as "an old sidekick."

She turned away from the glass and looked around the interior of the concrete-block structure. The outer office reminded her of a small-town bus station. An empty one. Why isn't anyone here to meet me? Where are the NASA security people Gonn promised? And transportation for Paul, wherever he needed to go? Red couldn't stay. But he could come back later if necessary; the *Star-News* office wasn't far. The pay phone on the wall was useless: rapidly repeating noise signaling busy circuits. A young officer had let Joni use a Navy line, but to no avail. The lady's voice had said, "Dr. Gonn will be unavailable indefinitely." Fishy as hell.

The Navy personnel on duty in the adjoining rooms had refused absolutely to comment on the supposed arrival of Paul's ship. She had not even been able to learn if any Coast Guard vessels were expected that afternoon. Resigned to a long wait, Joni paced back and forth by the windows. Now it was 1:35. She stopped again to look out. A long snowdrift off the corner of the building formed a ridge trailing toward the southwest. A short distance beyond it were two darker shapes which she had noticed on her way in: some sort of tanklike vehicles. Two dark shapes. She thought of her pursuers. I hope that guy by the

Capitol wasn't badly hurt. What could they have wanted from me? To stop me . . . stop me from meeting Paul? She held her breath. My God, that *must* be it! It's the only reason that makes any sense. But who were they? And why?

At length Joni walked over to a shelf against the back wall of the room where she had noticed a small portable radio. She tuned it to a continuous-news station for the latest reports. The clock showed 1:43. As soon as she had raised the volume to an audible level, an officer hurried in from the connecting communications office and waved his hand. "I'm sorry, miss, but we can't let you play that in here."

Slightly annoyed, she turned it off and asked, "How come? This transistor won't cause any interference." The crackle of radio static played in the background.

"Solid-state circuitry is funny," he replied patronizingly. "You never know what kind of . . . ah, stray frequencies you might get." She pursed her lips slightly to show that she hadn't been impressed by his explanation. "Anyway," he continued, "it's against the rules." He pivoted and marched off. Pausing in the open doorway, he glanced back and grinned. Smug bastard.

Joni watched him walk back into the next room. Another officer beckoned to him. The first one leaned over for a confidential message, then straightened up and spoke to someone she couldn't see. There were rustling and flopping noises, and Joni noticed the first officer eyeing her with a concerned expression. Suddenly, two men in fur-lined parkas and yellow boots appeared. They stomped past her without looking and rushed outside. She checked her watch: 1:47.

Joni grabbed her own parka. She had a hunch.

Zzzzzip! She forced her way out into the gale of snow and followed the vanishing figures toward the docks. Trudging through the drifts for even a few yards was a chore. She stopped before the first pier, where the two men had disappeared. She didn't want to be discovered and ordered away. Straining to see through the snow, she sensed motion on the right. Through the billowing clouds it was difficult to be sure if the movement had been real or imagined. Wait . . . yes. Yes! Something was moving, taking form.

The white hull of a ghost ship pushed through the sweeping snow. Joni's excitement throbbed in her ears. As she edged closer, she could see a diagonal red stripe and the numbers 1, 3, and 8 on the starboard bow. In a few moments, deck hands jumped to the pier and began securing lines from the rolling ship. A gangplank was lowered and . . . one, two, three figures came down.

The one in the middle joined the two men she had followed. This trio turned and began walking rapidly toward her as the others watched from the ramp. Joni stepped slightly to the side so that she wouldn't block their path, but she stayed close enough to see faces. As the vague figures approached and acquired detail, she squinted and tried to make them out. All three looked the same under parka hoods and behind goggles. Closer. The one in the middle could be Paul. It could be. Hands behind his back? Handcuffed? "Paul . . . Paul?" she cried.

His face turned; Joni knew the mouth. It shouted, "I'm under arrest . . . got to get me out!" As soon as he had started to speak, the men flanking him had shoved forward to prevent further conversation. Joni trotted after them. Paul looked over his shoulder and yelled, ". . . storm is man-made!" She could barely hear in the wind.

Storm is man-made. Joni repeated the phrase in her mind and slowed to a mechanical walk. That could have only one meaning. She didn't understand it, but it could have only one meaning. She was shocked by the implications.

Paul and his captors were nearly out of sight. Joni plunged into a laborious run to catch up, but they had put him onto one of the tanklike vehicles and powered away over the snow before she could get close enough to speak again. She stopped. Paul was gone. She had promised to meet him because he felt threatened. And she had been unable to help. Feeling the sinking ache of sudden disappointment, she turned and slogged back to the dock house.

She believed Paul. Now she knew the cause of his urgency. Perspiring from exertion and excitement, Joni took off her parka and threw it on the desk. She stared at the clock, momentarily uncertain about what to do. Abruptly, she turned and strode into the communications room. She addressed the officer who had told her to turn off the radio. "I am a friend of the man who was just taken away on that snow vehicle. His name is Paul Garfield and he had asked me to meet him." Joni nervously took out and presented her press card. "Before he was forcibly removed, he was able to tell me that he had been arrested. I should like to know who arrested him, why he is under arrest, and where he has been taken."

The young officer returned her credentials and shrugged. "I'm sorry, miss, I don't know anything about it. I'm afraid I can't help you."

"Oh, sure. And I suppose you didn't know that

ship was coming in either. Look, Dr. Garfield is a private citizen on an important mission. I hope you realize that this so-called arrest amounts to illegal abduction." Her voice was tense. "You have no right to deny me the information." Two enlisted men sitting in front of radio equipment turned to watch.

"I don't know about that, lady," the officer replied. "You're on Navy property, you know." He was becoming defensive.

"Well, you *will* know about it if I don't get some cooperation. You'd better believe that I can get this affair investigated right from the top. What's happened here is an outrage. Now, *where* has Dr. Garfield been taken?" she demanded.

"I told you, I'm not sure." He was weakening. He tightened his Navy necktie. "But I think that the prisoner is to be held in the Yard—at least temporarily. Probably till the storm quits."

"May I use your phone again?"

"No, I'm sorry, miss. My orders prohibit private calls."

"But you let me use it earlier," Joni protested.

"I'm sorry. Those are my orders."

"May I have your name and rank?" Joni was angry.

"Yes." He hesitated. "Ensign Allison T. Hornaday."

Joni turned away and marched back across the outer room directly to the pay phone. She moved with nervous quickness. Coins: ding-ding, dong. The circuits were busy. She punched the buttons again: still busy. She wished that she had called David sooner. She would keep trying until she got through.

David Bradford was sitting at his dining-room table, holding a cup of coffee and gazing into the

171

back yard. Swirling clouds of snowflakes gusted from the roof and filled his view. For him the whirling whiteness was more than mildly mesmerizing.

He might have been in northeast Denver staring through his bedroom window at the street light in front of the family house. A twelve-year-old boy filled with excitement, watching the snow and urging it on. He had watched the flakes float past that street light half the night, wishing away the hours till train time. The Moffat Tunnel train to Winter Park and the ski slopes. There wasn't another junior-high kid in the state that could keep close to him downhill. Flakes and flakes and flakes.

Snow had always held a hypnotic allure for him, the same kind of perpetual fascination that others find in flickering flame or rolling surf. He had a private relationship with snow. He spoke to it now in his thoughts the way he used to do out loud, as one would to an old and intimate friend. But this unceasing snowstorm seemed aloof—an alien giant. Something was different. He had been away from the snow too long, he supposed. "More coffee?"

The Senator had heard something. "What?"

"David, I asked if you would like more coffee."

"Oh. No . . . no thanks." He smiled benignly up at his wife, Carla. Looking back out the window, he slowly shook his head. "This storm is unbelievable."

"Well, if you're finished with your lunch, maybe you'd better try to do something about all that water in the basement."

"Okay. Right away." He stood up and started down the hallway toward the bathroom. The telephone rang.

Carla answered, "Hello?"

"May I please speak with Senator Bradford?"

"Who's calling, please?" Carla pretended. She had recognized the voice.

"Joni Dubin."

"I'm afraid the Senator can't come to the telephone right now, Miss Dubin. May I take a message?"

"It's a matter of the utmost urgency. I'm certain that he would want to know about it."

"Well, may I take the message?"

"There is quite a bit of information. If at all possible, I am sure that the Senator would want to receive it directly. This is an extremely serious matter."

"Very well, just a moment. I think he's in the basement. We're having a flooding problem because of this blizzard." Joni wanted to smile at that, but was too upset.

"I am *not* in the basement." The Senator returned from the hallway. "Who is that?" Carla handed him the phone with a jerk and a frown. "This is David Bradford."

"Hello, David. It's Joni. I hope I'm not disturbing you."

"Oh, hello, Miss Dubin. No, not at all. I suppose you're snowed in like the rest of us?"

"Yes, I am, but you'd never guess where." Before he could reply, she continued. "I had a terrible time reaching you. Busy circuits. I've been calling continually for ten minutes."

"Oh, I'm sorry to hear that. What's on your mind?" Carla was standing in the kitchen doorway with her arms folded.

"David," Joni sounded alarmed, "they're telling me

to get off, so I'll have to make it quick. I need your help."

"You know you can count on that."

"Paul's in trouble. He . . ." There was a pause. Senator Bradford could hear her speaking away from the phone. "Just one more minute," she shouted. Then her voice came back to him. "I don't have much time. Ready for some fast talk?"

"Go."

"I didn't tell you this morning, but Paul phoned late last night. Said he was coming from New York on a Coast Guard ship and asked me to meet him. He said to keep it confidential, that it was urgent. More than Conroy—a matter of national security." At this revelation the Senator frowned and began massaging his head. He knew about the emergency meeting of the National Security Council.

"I'm at the Washington Navy Yard by the docks," Joni explained. "Paul just arrived, but he's been arrested, and I can't . . ."

The Senator heard a clank and rustling noises. "Stop it! Goddam you," she screamed. "David, they're taking the phone. Paul said this storm is man-made. You've got to free him! He's being held somewhere here . . ."

The Senator wanted to ask questions. There was a lot to sort out and no time. But he had the meaning. "Stay there, Joni. I'll get you both to my office. . . . Joni?"

The phone was humming a dial tone. Holding it absently, he stared at the raging snowstorm outside.

"What's going on?" Carla wanted to know.

"Trouble." He replaced the receiver. "I've got to

think"—his code phrase requesting privacy. He put his hands in his pockets and walked to the dining-room window.

"David, you're not going out in this blizzard?"

17

~~~~~~

WASHINGTON NATIONAL AIRPORT:
6:00 PM, FRIDAY, DECEMBER 22

TEMPERATURE: 23°F

BAROMETER: 28.70″ (FALLING)

WIND: NE 40–60 MPH

SNOW DEPTH: 4′2″ (DRIFTS TO 15′)

FORECAST: SNOW ENDING TONIGHT,
CLEARING AND COLDER

Curtis Zimber studied himself in the lavatory mirror.
The strong brown eyes were circled and bloodshot.
His face looked old and tired in the guileless
fluorescent light. And he could find less of his father's

presence in it than before; the reassuring paternal power seemed diminished, drained.

The Admiral was preparing to shave in the bathroom of his Pentagon office. After dipping his badger-hair brush into the water and swishing it around in a wooden soap dish, he applied the lather to his face and neck. Then, turning his chin up to the right, he carefully scraped the sharp steel of a straight-edged razor across the rough skin of his throat. The instrument's handle bore the faded initials "K.Z.," those of his father, Konrad Zimber. The reflection of Walter Popowski appeared at the side of the mirror. The Admiral's assistant had just entered the inner office behind him. "Well, come on," Zimber spluttered through the soap. "Where are they now?"

"Still a hundred and forty miles north of the center," Popowski replied.

"Christ, what's the holdup this time?"

Popowski was examining a sheaf of papers. His hands were trembling. "They're just having a hell of a rough time. Taking twenty-foot waves and winds gusting to seventy knots. *Manatee* can't push it any faster."

"Oooh! . . . Fuckin' razor's getting dull." The Admiral touched a face cloth to the cut on his cheek. "They're probably exaggerating."

"Exaggerating or not, they're reaching the limit of what that ship can take. After all, it's a research vessel, not a hurricane wagon."

"So maybe Rodek should go down now." Zimber undertook the delicate operation of slicing stubble from around the corners of his nose.

"Not enough fuel," Popowski explained. "*Nessie*

177

needs to be within a hundred nautical miles." He sank into the Admiral's couch, visibly fatigued.

Zimber wiped remnants of lather from his face. He paused, again searching his own eyes. Then he turned and walked into the office, carrying a face towel. He sighed heavily, "You know, Walter, I shouldn't't've been so goddam greedy. I wish I were retired and down on my island, out fishing on *Mariah*."

The Admiral ambled over to the window and looked out into the storm. "You try to do something innovative and important for your country, make your mark with something you believe in. You take care of yourself a little, and your friends. And you wind up in a tub of shit!"

Popowski was staring at the floor. "We've had some incredibly bad luck, Curtis."

"Or some interference." Zimber turned and walked back to his desk. "Any word yet on the Soviet inquiry?"

"None. I'd have told you immediately."

"Fuck!" The Admiral threw down his towel. "We had everything under control. Got around all the pussyfoots. Plugged the leaks. Double-checked the system. Then it all starts comin' unglued. An entire career." He glanced at Popowski. "Know what my wife would say if she knew about this mess?"

"Sir?" Walter looked up.

"Same old shit. That I shoulda listened to her. The I-told-you-so routine." He sat down and picked up a cigar, rotating it slowly in his fingers. "She and I haven't understood each other for years. There's no closeness."

Popowski folded his arms and took a deep breath.

Admiral Zimber rarely discussed his marraige—except to complain that his wife drank too much.

"She always claimed I was trying to live up to some myth I had about my father," Zimber continued. "That I had to prove my manhood through conquest and domination. The 'Hemingway macho mystique,' she calls it. I figured she picked that stuff up from some shrink. She said that conquering external things was a boy's substitute for conquering self. She even resented my deep-sea fishing. Hell," he shrugged, "maybe she's right. Sometimes I think so. The whole fuckin' world is meaningless. My *life!*" Zimber stood up and stalked back to the bathroom. "I'm sick to death of worrying about it. If we can pull this outa the fire, I'll be more than content to go conquer a marlin. I'm ready to escape."

A red telephone rang behind the Admiral's desk. "Code circuit, Admiral," announced Popowski, pulling himself to his feet.

"You get it.

"Admiral Zimber's office, Popowski speaking." He listened; then, "Just a minute." He held his palm over the mouthpiece and glanced up. "It's Singer at special security. Want to talk?"

Zimber was cleaning his razor. "Naah, go ahead."

"I'll take it." Popowski listened again and frowned even more than usual. "You can be *damn* sure he's not going to like it," he exclaimed.

The Admiral turned. "What's that? *What* am I not going to like?"

"Garfield's been sprung."

Curtis Zimber stared at his assistant, his eyes seeming to enlarge and become more rounded. "How?" he shouted.

"Direct orders from the Secretary of the Navy."

"What? How did that asshole get involved?"

Popowski spoke again into the telephone. "You heard?" In a moment he looked up. "At the request of the Vice President. Garfield's been released to the custody of Senator Bradford."

"Holy shit! That Black pain in the ass. More trouble than he's fuckin' worth." He hesitated, then, "Where'd they take Garfield?"

"Bradford's office."

"Jesus Christ! All we need is for him to . . . What time is that next NSC meeting?"

"Eight o'clock," Popowski replied.

"No fuckin' time for *anything!*" Zimber's face was flushed and shaking with intensity. "Now hear this: we just confirmed that Garfield is an enemy agent. An assassin." He thrust out the straight-edged razor and waved it erratically at Walter Popowski. "Kill him," he said slowly. "No questions. Kill him now. And it wouldn't be too bad if Bradford got wasted 'by accident' in the process."

The clock on Senator Bradford's desk showed 7:15. The Senator leaned back in his chair as he talked to Joni Dubin, who was standing near the window holding a cup of coffee. Relaxed now, after her frantic afternoon, she was rosy-cheeked and full of enthusiasm as she said, "That's right: Ensign Allison T. Hornaday. I wish I could describe his expression when he came in to tell me that Paul would be released and that they were going to furnish us transportation to your office. He and another officer drove us all the way on the same kind of contraption they used to abduct Paul."

180

"After what you two went through," the Senator confessed, "I almost feel guilty for having been able to come most of the way underground. I have never seen a blizzard as severe as this one—not even above timberline." He turned to his assistant, who had just arrived. "Did you have any trouble, Frank?"

"No sir. It is unbelievably bad outside, but the Metro pass you requested was in order and waiting for me." Frank was sitting at the side of the desk on David Bradford's right; he held a large briefcase in his lap. "Where is Dr. Garfield now?" he asked.

"He went to the shower room to clean up and change clothes," Senator Bradford replied. "He was in pretty miserable shape after that trip he had. And now he's got to walk into the lions' den at the White House."

"Those Navy people didn't help much," Joni added. "They treated him like some kind of criminal. Me too, for that matter. I was really furious. But after the release order, I decided not to rock the boat. I became so docile and polite they could hardly stand it. Losing in one-upmanship seems to bother military people more than—"

Someone was knocking at the door. "That must be Paul. Will you let him in, Frank?" the Senator asked.

Still clutching the briefcase, Frank jumped up and unlocked the door to the outer office. A pale Paul Garfield stepped in. Frank could see two men in topcoats standing in the reception area as he reclosed the door.

Joni put down her cup and hurried over to greet Paul. "Feeling better?" She took his hand.

"Yes, finally." He smiled weakly. "I think my gut can handle that milk now."

David Bradford immediately rose and walked to his refrigerator cabinet. "Are you sure you don't want me to try to find a doctor before we go?" he inquired.

"No, I'll be all right, David. Besides, there isn't time. If I feel queasy, we can ask for medication at the White House. They should be well stocked with tranquilizers."

"Paul," said Joni, "this is Frank Taylor, the young man I mentioned who has been helping David with his investigations."

"Hi." Paul shook his hand. "I hear you've got some pretty heavy stuff."

"It's a pleasure to meet you, Dr. Garfield." He hefted his briefcase. "Yes, in fact I have some of the more pertinent material right here."

Senator Bradford approached them and handed Paul a glass of milk. "Of course, Frank is not yet aware of your information, Paul. When we're able to tell him, I'm sure he'll be as amazed as I was to learn where some of our tentative findings were leading."

"Circumstantial as your evidence may be, David," Paul was emphatic, "we may need it to make a convincing presentation. The story's just so damn fantastic. And, as you well know, Zimber's got a lot of influence and a lot of believers. Heads will be on the block, so the powers that be may require considerable persuading."

"I'll be ready and willing—eager—to back you up, Paul," the Senator assured him, nodding toward Frank and his briefcase.

"It seems to me that they don't have much choice other than to believe you at this point," Joni commented.

"The incredible thing," Paul observed, sipping his

milk, "is how men like Zimber lose all sense of proportion and perspective. And Berger's no better. I mean, just consider what the relative stakes are." He was walking toward the window. "The necks of a few individuals versus a major catastrophe and a confrontation between two superpowers." He gazed through the glass. The dim glow of street lamps below seemed to be coming from a very great distance, diminished by obscuring matter in intervening space. Ancient light from dying suns.

David Bradford glanced at his watch. "We'd better get ready to go. Vice President Lindemann has arranged for us to speak to the President immediately before the start of the National Security Council meeting. Once he hears what you have to say, Paul, you'll undoubtedly preempt the rest of the agenda." He motioned toward the door. "Mrs. Lindemann also sent over the two Secret Service agents out front to escort us. Thank God for her friendship and confidence; without them, everything would've been much slower and more difficult."

"And thank God for the Secret Service." Paul put down his empty milk glass and turned away from the window. "We'll be in danger until we've told our full story; Zimber has got to be desperate by now. The only thing my involvement in this has cost me so far is my job and reputation when I quit the project—and last night's dinner. But Joni and I were lucky today. We could easily have disappeared like John Conroy."

"David, is there any news about that?" queried Joni with a worried expression.

"Still nothing. Naturally, Mrs. Conroy is very worried. She's home, waiting."

The Senator pushed the intercom button on his desk. We're ready, gentlemen." He looked up. "Here's the plan. We'll go belowground to Union Station, where we'll take the subway to Metro Center. There we'll transfer to a special car, which will stop in mid-tunnel at the north end of the Treasury building. From there, we'll enter the emergency Secret Service access and walk underground through Treasury and across into the White House."

Paul Garfield sighed and pulled a pack of cigarettes from his borrowed trousers. "I guess I'll start smoking again."

"What's keeping that special train?" worried David Bradford as he looked at his watch. It was 7:43. He turned to Paul Garfield. "We should *be* there now." They were standing on a trackside platform near the west end of the Metro Center station.

"Excuse me, Senator Bradford." One of their two Secret Service escorts approached him. "I just spoke to the White House. Our Metro car is on its way; it had to wait for another train to clear the line. We should be in the West Wing in ten minutes."

"So they know that Dr. Garfield is en route?" inquired Joni Dubin, who was standing between Bradford and Frank Taylor.

"Yes, ma'am," the tall, freckle-faced agent assured her. "And, Senator, I understand that the NSC meeting is expected to start slightly behind schedule."

Joni smiled at Paul. "I'm sure the President will see you even if we're a little late. David told Elizabeth Lindemann that your report was of the highest priority."

"I know, but in an emergency like this, highest

184

priorities are a dime a dozen. The problem is to get attention and be believed."

Although it was cold in the cavernous tunnel, Paul started pulling out of his parka. Joni helped him. "Nervous?" she asked.

"Sure." He folded the coat on his arm and glanced around the platform.

There were relatively few people in this section of the station. A dozen or so reporters and photographers huddled nearby, chatting animatedly. They had recognized Senator Bradford and Joni Dubin immediately upon arrival, but had temporarily suspended their questioning after repeated replies of "no comment" and conciliatory photographs. They hadn't recognized Paul.

A platoon of marines in winter combat dress stood at rest along the far wall, while Metro and District of Columbia police diligently guarded the escalators, overhanging landings, and tunnel interchanges. A few subway employees and other persons in civilian dress were scattered across the platforms on both sides of the tracks. The background murmur of crowd noise filtered down from the upper levels of the complex.

"There must be a lot of people stranded upstairs," Joni commented. "I'm surprised there aren't more down here."

"No unauthorized personnel are permitted at trackside, ma'am," the freckled agent explained.

Maintenance engineer Tyrone Simpson was examining a plan of Metro Center ventilation ducts. He stood near the tunnel wall about 150 feet down the platform from Paul Garfield and David Bradford. Suddenly he held his breath. What was that? Only two months after duck season, he wasn't about to mistake the sound of an engaging shotgun barrel. He listened. Clock Stock fore-end clamping under the barrel? Other noises: his heart, background chatter, faint metallic clicking, and a singularly distinctive *chwack!* Someone had just closed a shotgun.

Slowly, he turned around. About thirty feet behind him, two men were turned toward the wall, forming a shielded triangle. An open tool case lay next to them. The one with his back to Tyrone wore a subway employee's jacket like his own and held an overcoat on his arm. Only part of the other man was visible, but Simpson could see a Metro badge on his breast pocket. Both men wore wading boots.

Tyrone turned, tucked his ventilation plans under his arm, and walked stiffly in the opposite direction. Trying to look casual, he gradually accelerated his pace. Senator Bradford and his companions were the closest people. The tall Secret Service agent saw Simpson approaching. As soon as their eyes met, the anxious engineer made straight for him.

"I think I can see the train lights," Joni shouted, peering into the tunnel.

"S-s-s-say, mister, do you . . . are any of y-you p-p-p-police officers?" Tyrone was unable to control his stutter when excited.

"I'm with the Secret Service." The tall agent was on his guard. His partner had moved closer to the tracks in anticipation of the train car's arrival. "What seems to be the trouble?"

"I heard s-s-s-somebody foolin' with a s-s-s-s-scatter gun." The two men Simpson had seen were now walking rapidly toward them along the edge of the platform. The first held his overcoat out in front of him. The agent readied his revolver. "Th-th-th-

there," Tyrone was pointing, "there they come n-n-n . . ."

At that moment the overcoat caught on the man's boot and pulled to the floor. Twelve-gauge over-and-under sawed off! The weapon began to rise as the agent knocked Simpson aside. Three shots exploded from his .38 Special. The second bullet ruptured the gunman's heart; the third cracked his collarbone, throwing his body to the platform. Both shotgun barrels detonated, blasting to the ceiling with concussive force.

The second man in boots had pulled a .45 automatic. He hollered, "Hold it! I'm special security. That man is an assassin!" He was pointing at Garfield.

"Bullshit," muttered the tall agent, now shielding Paul. "Get down!" Frank stepped in front of David Bradford as the other Secret Service man aimed his revolver from trackside.

All three guns erupted in a deafening barrage. Joni Dubin screamed. The tall agent and the man with the .45 collapsed and died. Holding a bullet wound in his thigh, Frank Taylor grimaced as he saw the dead agent's freckled face sag into liquid red. Policemen and reporters and photographers were running.

At the edge of the platform, the second gunman's body kicked spasmodically, turned slowly over, and dropped. Sprawled across the tracks, its hand still clenched the .45. Three inches to the right, a sign warned in black on red: 750 VOLTS. The arm jerked, thrusting the steel pistol against the electric rail. Reports from unspent bullets punctuated the electrical pyrotechnics. The special Metro car jerked to a halt before the smoking corpse. And cameras clicked as flashes of magnesium light brightened the scene for posterity.

18

WASHINGTON NATIONAL AIRPORT:
8:00 PM, FRIDAY, DECEMBER 22

TEMPERATURE: 23°F

BAROMETER: 28.65″ (FALLING)

WIND: NE 40–65 MPH

SNOW DEPTH: 4′6″ (DRIFTS TO 19′)

FORECAST: SNOW ENDING TONIGHT,
CLEARING AND COLDER

"The Secretary of State is recognized." The President almost had to shout to make himself heard over the hubbub of background talk in the Cabinet Room. The chamber was considerably more crowded

189

than it had been during the afternoon meeting of the National Security Council. Eighteen people now lined the elliptical conference table, and a dozen more, including the Speaker of the House of Representatives and the majority and minority leaders of the House and Senate, sat in chairs around the walls of the room. Newcomers other than the Congressional leaders were deputies and assistants to Council members, plus invited experts and witnesses representing a variety of governmental agencies.

Conversations subsided as Secretary of State Kroner rose to speak. "Thank you, Mr. President. As many of you have probably learned, less than an hour ago we received from the Soviet Union an indignant, categorical denial of involvement in the modification of this storm."

"The louder they shout, the more they're lying," assessed CIA Director Satin. "Electronic surveillance continues to show an abnormally high level of Soviet activity out there."

"Moreover," Secretary Kroner continued, ignoring the interruption, "the U.S.S.R. has called for an emergency meeting of the United Nations Security Council to protest treaty violations which they allege *we* are effectuating in order to precipitate an international crisis." Whispering conversations resumed throughout the room; this development had not been generally known.

"Now there's the pot callin' the kettle black if I *ever* heard it! Absolutely incredible," exclaimed General Wilcox, Chairman of the Joint Chiefs. "That's what we get for waiting and depending on good faith!"

"Of course, there is no possibility of any U.N.

meeting now, and there probably won't be for at least several days." Secretary Kroner paused and pulled off his glasses. "Unfortunately, the Soviets included in their statement not one word of explanation regarding the May Day satellites or the ships clustered in the storm area. As a result, I am inclined to question their denial of responsibility." Frowning, he sank slowly into his chair. The Secretary's well-known propensity for caution and understatement served to underscore the seriousness of his conclusion.

"You're damn right!" Secretary of Defense Norris slammed down his pipe. "We can't afford to wait for more reports. Thousands of people are dying because of this thing—this 'Great American Blizzard' as it's called in the press. It's already a national disaster. We've got to get it stopped—and fast! As a first step, I call for the immediate declaration of a National Emergency and placement of our worldwide military forces on full alert."

"Second!" assented Director Satin.

"That will require advising the Soviet Chairman in advance via the Hot Line," said Secretary Kroner. "We can allow no possibility of their misinterpreting our intentions."

General Wilcox rose from his chair. "That is correct, Mr. Secretary. We should set a short-term deadline for follow-up action so there *can* be no misinterpretation." He turned to the President. "As a second step in conjunction with Secretary Norris's proposal, I recommend that we issue an ultimatum on the Hot Line threatening to sever diplomatic relations and to take military action if the Russians do not cease all activities in the storm area by midnight our time tonight. We should also demand a full explanation of what they've been doing. As per—"

"General Wilcox," interrupted the Secretary of State.

"Please let me finish, Kroner." The General heaved a deep breath. "As per the attack plan I presented this afternoon, we're ready to go in and blow those Russian trawlers and subs out of the water and to destroy their May Day satellites with nuclear missiles." The Cabinet Room was quiet as the General sat down.

Trembling and flushed, Secretary of State Kroner addressed the Chief Executive. "Mr. President, General Wilcox's approach is tantamount to a declaration of war. A choice between the present predicament and global incineration is hardly what we seek. I-I . . ." Stammering slightly, he paused to clear his throat. "In the first place, severing diplomatic relations would be pointless—self-defeating. We should keep all lines of communication open.

"Secondly, I cannot agree to the words, or even the sense of the words, 'ultimatum' and 'threaten.' Particularly involving military action. We must avoid forcing the Soviets into a corner from which they might react instinctively in their own defense." He glanced at the Chairman of the Joint Chiefs, then back at the President.

"It's a matter of basic psychology. As in the handling of the Cuban missile crisis, we should apply pressure while allowing the Soviets a means of saving face."

The President nodded in agreement. "Your points are well taken, Charles."

General Wilcox slapped his palm flat on the table. "All right. Soften the language. Just so the meaning is clear and we're ready to move."

Some of the pressure of intense discussion had been relieved, and the room suddenly became noisy. The President stood up and raised his hand for silence.

"Is it the will of the Council," he asked solemnly, "to follow the recommendations of Secretary Norris and General Wilcox as amended by Secretary Kroner? I can tell you that I am now disposed to do so."

There was a mixture of affirmative replies. Of the regular Council members, only the Vice President remained silent. "Are there any dissenting views?" the Chief Executive inquired. His tone suggested that he wished there were. "You all understand, of course," the President went on, "that this course of action will be implemented immediately." He was gripping the edge of the table to keep his hands from shaking. "I also remind you that National Emergency status authorizes me to institute federalized martial law throughout the regions designated National Disaster Areas. This is in agreement with recommendations made by the Domestic Council this afternoon."

The President waited for a moment. Then he announced, "Very well. Consider the decision made." He beckoned for Wilson Keithley-Smythe, his National Security Advisor. After a short conversation, Keithley-Smythe and Herbert Salisbury hurried out of the room. The President again addressed the Council. "The plan is in motion. My interpreters are ready. As soon as the Soviet Chairman has acknowledged our Hot Line request, I will interrupt the meeting to apprise him of our position." Behind the

President on the mantlepiece, the clock read 8:25.

A few minutes later, Herbert Salisbury reentered the room and approached the President with a message.

19

~~~~~~

WASHINGTON NATIONAL AIRPORT:
  8:00 PM, FRIDAY, DECEMBER 22

TEMPERATURE: 23°F

BAROMETER: 28.65″ (FALLING)

WIND: NE 40–65 MPH

SNOW DEPTH: 4′6″ (DRIFTS TO 19′)

FORECAST: SNOW ENDING TONIGHT,
  CLEARING AND COLDER

The clock had advanced to 8:36. "He's under incredible pressure," noted Defense Secretary Norris, holding his pipe in his mouth. "Just be glad you didn't have to make the call."

"Of course he is, but so are we," complained the

Secretary of State. "He might have given us some word about the tone of the acknowledgment." Five minutes earlier, the President and the Vice President had exited the Cabinet Room without comment in the company of Herbert Salisbury. "What we're doing is frighteningly risky," the Secretary added.

"Maybe not as risky as you think, Charlie." Secretary Norris was staring thoughtfully at the pad in front of him. "You've got to be prepared to go to the line, but that doesn't mean you'll ever have to cross it. Especially in a situation of balance. A willingness to go helps assure that your adversary won't cross either. Ultimately, that's the only means of maintaining your relative positions. To avoid confrontation regardless of circumstances is to signal weakness. I like to think of it as a sort of ritual testing of dominance."

"You make us sound like pack animals," Kroner protested.

"Or poker players," Norris returned.

"Well, Lloyd, perhaps my instincts are hopelessly civilized." A door opened, causing Secretary Kroner to look around. "Now who in the world are those . . . isn't that Senator Bradford?"

"Yes, it certainly is." The Defense Secretary frowned. "And the girl is that television reporter . . . what's-her-name. We might as well throw these meetings open to the public."

The President followed Vice President Lindemann, Herbert Salisbury, and the two newcomers into the Cabinet Room. Agitated voices behind them were cut off when the door shut. Their arrival stimulated much murmuring speculation. The Chief Executive ushered Joni Dubin and the Senator to chairs by the windows, next to the minority and majority leaders of the Senate. David Bradford shook hands and exchanged perfunctory greetings with both men. Joni nodded politely, eschewing formal introduction. With a quick gesture, the President tendered his place at the head of the table to the Vice President, and he and Herbert Salisbury sat down.

Mrs. Lindemann stood stiffly and glanced around the room, waiting for silence. In a moment she commanded her audience. Her voice was sharp, almost brittle. "An extraordinary sequence of events today—in which I played an accidental and minor role—has brought us a critically important witness. Sufficiently important for the President to have instructed Mr. Keithley-Smythe to suspend preliminary communication on the Hot Line. For the purpose of introducing this witness, I present Senator David Winslow Bradford of the State of Colorado, who has been instrumental in bringing him to us." The Vice President promptly yielded the floor. The room was quiet.

"Thank you, Madam Vice President." The youthful Senator's voice trembled slightly, more from emotion than nervousness. "Dr. Paul Garfield," he began, extending his hand toward Paul, "will reveal facts so fantastic that you may at first find them difficult to believe. But his report is of paramount importance to the current crisis. Having known him personally, I can vouch with full confidence for his veracity, and I am able to support some of his assertions with evidence uncovered by my own investigations. That aside, I am certain that Dr. Garfield will quickly establish his credibility."

"He finds himself in the unenviable position of

having to expose an example of bad judgment and conspiracy so extreme that it has brought our country to the verge of disaster. Moreover, he has come to us at great personal risk, literally at the risk of his life. Within the hour," the Senator's voice broke, "two misguided assassins attempted to prevent his reaching this Council. I regret to say that a Secret Service agent was shot to death in that encounter, and that one of my own assistants was wounded." Whispers of surprise and uncertainty hissed in the background. Bradford paused, clasping his hands in front of him and looking down at the table, almost as if in prayer. Then he looked up.

"For many years, Dr. Garfield has distinguished himself as an astrophysicist and applied meteorologist, first at the National Center for Atmospheric Research, then with the National Aeronautics and Space Administration and the Office of Naval Research. More recently, he has been teaching at Columbia University." The Senator hesitated, glancing at Joni Dubin.

"I should point out that because, more than anyone else, she made it possible for Dr. Garfield to come here, and because she is already aware of what he has to say, the President has given Miss Joni Dubin, who is well known to most of us for her work in television, special permission to sit in on this meeting. Of course, she had pledged absolute confidence. I am grateful to the President for granting me the same permission. I now give you Dr. Paul Garfield for his testimony."

"Forgive me for asking, Mr. President," interjected CIA Director Satin, "but, in view of the urgency of the situation, are you totally convinced of the relevance of this testimony and of the . . . uh, confidence of these visitors?"

"Yes," the President replied sharply. "Dr. Garfield, please proceed." Wilson Keithley-Smythe reentered the room, spoke a few words to the President, and sat down in his chair on the near left.

Paul rose and moved to the head of the imposing table. In David Bradford's shirt and pants, his dress was conspicuously casual. But his nervous manner betrayed his self-consciousness and apprehension. He was perspiring; his pulse was pounding. He might have been facing his first class, one he feared would consist entirely of cynical, hostile students. He glanced over at David Bradford, who had returned to his chair next to Joni Dubin.

"Thank you, Senator Bradford." He turned to the President and Vice President on his right. "I sincerely appreciate having the opportunity to address the Council. I believe that what I have to say is of the utmost importance to your deliberations." Now looking out over the long table surrounded by intense faces, "I intend to present my thesis first, and then to review pertinent background information. Please interrupt me with questions at any time." Paul had rehearsed his opening remarks many times in his mind. And he had unconsciously reverted to his novitiate lecturing style.

"We're listening, son," General Wilcox assured him as he removed the cellophane wrapper from a cheap cigar.

Paul took a deep breath and tried to fix as many pairs of eyes as he could while speaking. "I am convinced that the catastrophic blizzard we are now experiencing—already twice as severe and extensive as any previously recorded winter storm—is not only man-made but is of our own making, not the Russians."

Shocked silence prevailed. Not one murmur. It was sinking-in time. The silence was broken by a burst from Chairman Wilcox. "That is absolutely preposterous!"

"It may be surprising, but it is not preposterous," Paul replied firmly, looking directly into the eyes of his challenger. Being put on the defensive had restored his courage. He took a pack of cigarettes from his shirt pocket, lit one, and laid the pack on the table before him.

"Now, see here—" General Wilcox began.

An incredulous President interrupted the confrontation. "Good God, man! I had no idea. Are you telling us that we are doing this to *ourselves*?!" The question hung in the air, seeming to repeat itself.

"Exactly." Paul glanced down, then looked back at the President for some sign of confidence. Excited talk was breaking out across the room.

"Horseshit," muttered Vincent Satin. "What's the basis for that wild charge?"

"It used to be my project." Paul paused, smoke streaming from his nostrils. He had just pleaded guilty before the jury.

He continued. "During the decline of the space program and the deflation of NASA, as Senator Bradford mentioned, I moved to the Office of Naval Research." Nodding at Defense Secretary Norris, "Your predecessor was my boss then. I proposed a series of experiments designed initially to modify the thermal influx to small tropical depressions—potential

200

storms. At first, our ideas were received with enthusiasm and the preliminary research was funded routinely. Weather-modification studies. Harmless enough *then*."

"Let's go to the bottom line," barked a scowling Chairman of the Joint Chiefs of Staff. Paul didn't expect to be called "son" again soon.

"Almost six years ago I developed the idea—with several colleagues—for a project we called 'Low Blow.' Fundamentally, it was a simple idea: put a cluster of nuclear reactors on the sea floor and, by remote control, activate them as heat sources. The concept was sound in principle, but the question was whether—"

"Dr. Garfield," interrupted the horn-rimmed Secretary of State, "you realize, of course, that such a venture at that time would have constituted a clear violation of the treaty prohibition against seabed devices?"

"Well, I wasn't sure. I had seen a general description of the treaty in the newspapers, but I assumed that it applied only to explosive devices, such as nuclear mines and suboceanic missile sites." Paul was hedging. It was on this point that he felt most vulnerable. Joni Dubin was watching him intently, as was everyone else in the room.

"In any case," he went on, "we were still in the research stage, and I was assured that the treaty was not relevant. Later, when I learned otherwise, my group was instructed to ignore it because the Russians were doing the same thing. Our security became extremely tight. The prevailing attitude seemed to be that covert or carefully disguised treaty violations were standard operating procedure."

201

"Not so," snapped Secretary Kroner.

"Yes, sir. I know that now. I must confess that, in those days, I considered such interpretations or decisions to be military-political—at least, not my responsibility." Paul was looking for an ash tray. Keithley-Smythe pushed one to him. "Unfortunately, I chose to believe what I was told, and I worked on my project."

"Sounds like something Werner von Braun might have said," commented Albert Kaufman, the President's science advisor.

"In my own defense," Paul responded, wiping his forehead, "full realization of the illegality of the project was a factor in my subsequent resignation. But initially I was a scientist dislodged from my niche at NASA, and I was searching for a new one. I became very much interested in weather modification. Because of the degree of my interest, my background, and the attractiveness of our proposal, I was appointed Director of the Suboceanic Weapons Investigation and Research Laboratory, SWIRL."

"We congratulate you for that, Dr. Garfield," proffered the Secretary of Defense sarcastically, "and we understand your defensiveness about the illegality of your project, but—with all due respect to Secretary Kroner—I think we've heard enough about treaty violations." The Secretary's voice was rising. "We've got a national emergency to deal with. What have you got to offer? You've made some pretty damn reckless charges here. Let's hear you support them. Let's have some hard evidence!"

"Yes, sir. But I feel that I must complete the background so that you'll understand what has happened and, frankly, so that you'll believe me." Paul cleared his throat. "Returning to Project Low Blow, we believed that if high-speed nuclear reactors were placed where normal oceanic currents are upward, then their enormous capacity for heat generation could be used to augment the normal vertical rise of warmer water. By arranging several reactors in a circular pattern, we hoped to create a rising ring of relatively hot water that would expand toward the surface in a conelike configuration."

"Very interesting," gibed General Wilcox, "but can you help us get a handle on the relevance of this to our problem? We don't have time for a technical lecture."

The Secretary of State pulled off his glasses and asked, "What does hot water have to do with a blizzard?"

The President tried to ease the pressure. "I am sure that Dr. Garfield will answer those questions shortly. Let's give him a chance."

Paul nodded in appreciation and continued. "By the time the warm-water cone intersected the ocean surface, we estimated that it would have spread out to a diameter of at least several miles. Its heat would in turn be transferred to the atmosphere above, feeding a rising funnel of warm, moist air that would turn counterclockwise because of the earth's rotation. Such a convection cell would have a built-in 'eye', thereby allowing for inward as well as outward movement of the displaced cooler air.

"Now we come to the application." Paul fingered blond hair back from his forehead and lit another cigarette. There was some background buzzing, but most of those in the room were listening carefully. "Although the heat output of high-speed reactors is very large by human standards, it is small compared to the necessary to drive even a minor natural storm.

"Accordingly, it was never our intention to try to induce a new atmospheric depression, but rather to enhance an existing center of low pressure. A weak one. To see if our small increment, distributed in a pattern designed for maximum efficiency, could make a difference—perhaps a critical difference—and trigger the development of a major storm. The artificial enhancement would have to be timed to coincide with the passage of a natural low. We thought that there was also a possibility of slowing the migration of such a storm, that one might even be held in position over our feeder funnel for a limited . . . really, an unknown period of time."

Paul's sincerity, obvious intelligence, and the clarity of his explanations were gradually winning him the confidence of his audience. And there was a growing understanding of the gravity of his disclosures. No longer was he being interrupted by skeptical or disparaging comments.

"But," he shrugged, "although the research looked promising, my project was not officially funded for development. Too sensitive. The seabed treaty we discussed earlier may have been the principal reason. I don't know. I do know that weather control—'weather warfare'—was under negotiation in the SALT talks. Since it was a subject of current attention, I suspect that it was the overriding factor. However, as has been suggested, we've probably spent too much time on treaties already."

Secretary of State Kroner leaned forward. "Now that you have given us the background and convinced us of your key role, for God's sake, what happened next and how could it have led us here?"

"To be brief, some people in the Department of the Navy thought it was a great idea and arranged to carry it with hidden, nonbudgeted funds—of which we all know there are literally billions expended annually."

"Leave me out of that," requested Defense Secretary Norris with a smug smile. "I don't know any such thing." He glanced around the table like a small boy looking for approval. At the side of the room, David Bradford frowned and cleared his throat exaggeratedly.

"It must have been an incredibly expensive project," exclaimed Dr. Kaufman. "Reactors constructed for submarine operation would cost a fortune."

"That is correct, sir," Paul confirmed. "I have reason to believe that much of the money came through the CIA."

"So do I," added Senator Bradford. The noise level rose immediately.

Vincent Satin jerked to his feet. "That's a goddam lie! Mr. President, I protest in the strongest possible terms. This is a crisis situation, not a forum for Bradford's opportunism. We're not here to listen to a bunch of contrived accusations."

"You're right. Calm down, Vincent. We'll discuss that later." The President looked up at Paul. "Will you continue your report on Project Low Blow? And never mind the funding." Director Satin sat down and glowered at Garfield.

Paul snubbed out his cigarette. His face was flushed. "I agreed to proceed with development in secret," he admitted, "but only to test the concept. To see if it would work. In cooperation with a special group from the Atomic Energy Commission, we obtained a source for the reactors. AEC didn't know what they were for. I think they were told that there was a classified project for underwater power generation. In any case, the reactors provided tremendous heat output. Controlled thermal pollution with military and nonmilitary potential.

"We sank the first series in barges two thousand meters in the northeast Pacific. It worked. And we had better control than we had anticipated. Enhancement was terminated after twelve hours, and the storm weakened and moved off. Six months later— without my consent or participation—another 'experiment' was conducted off Cuba. A minor tropical depression grew into a hurricane that hugged their coast for a week and totally destroyed the annual sugar corp. Hundreds of thousands of people suffered because of it. I felt responsible like . . . well, like Fermi after Hiroshima, I suppose."

"Oh come now, Dr. Garfield. We understand your concern, but please do not take the occasion of this disaster to flatter yourself." General Wilcox.

The inappropriateness of the General's remark was indicative of the mounting tension. "I could not tolerate such gross misuse of my project," Paul went on, unruffled. "I could not then, and I cannot now. What? Experiment with the lives of entire peoples or countries? I have no desire to play God. Unfortunately, some do." He paused. There was a lot of throat-clearing but no challenge.

"How many reactors were used in the Caribbean?" queried Dr. Kaufman.

"Six. Disguised as bauxite barges and sunk at night."

"Six," repeated Secretary Kroner. "Like the points of a snowflake."

"Yes, I suppose so," Paul affirmed impatiently. He sighed. "So, in that Cuban experiment, my trust had been violated. I had developed the system as a potential resource, not for covert military or political application." He was looking at the ceiling, as though talking to himself. He had held in these feelings for a long time. It was clear to many of those present that Paul's testimony was as much an expurgation of personal guilt as it was an exposé of malfeasance. Joni Dubin had been staring at him steadily, hoping to catch his eye so that she could give him a special smile of approval and reassurance. But he had avoided looking at her, afraid of what he might see.

"No sooner did we show that it would work, than the bastards took all control of it away from me." Paul looked at the President. "I suppose I should've foreseen that. I bailed out of the project, out of ONR, and out of Civil Service altogether." Paul suddenly realized that his voice was much louder than it needed to be.

He hesitated for a moment, then continued more softly. "I let it be known that if my project were ever used again for destructive purposes or dangerous experimentation, I would blow the whistle. For a number of reasons, I am convinced that this blizzard is a runaway result of the latest test." Another pregnant pause, and another cigarette.

"So, here I am. But, as Senator Bradford pointed out, it has not been easy. Those responsible for this are unprincipled and desperate men. First they arrested me, then they tried to kill me. One of my former colleagues has disappeared—probably killed. I have no doubt that you'll be told—perhaps you already have been—that I'm a foreign agent or insane." He inhaled.

"My conclusion is that they wanted to test the system on a little winter storm, and that it has somehow gotten wildy out of control." Paul stopped. He had made his speech.

Turning to the side, he exhaled in relief and tried a smoke ring. Damned if it wasn't perfect: a swirling white circle. Behind it, growing snowdrifts had completely blocked the ten-foot-high, doubly insulated windows of the Cabinet Room.

The President straightened up in his chair. "At least this is a beginning. Thank God we didn't go farther with the Soviets. But now that we know where the responsibility lies, how in the world could this operation have gotten out of control, and what in *hell* can we do about it?"

20

WASHINGTON NATIONAL AIRPORT:
9:00 PM, FRIDAY, DECEMBER 22

TEMPERATURE: 23°F

BAROMETER: 28.62″ (FALLING)

WIND: NE 40–70 MPH

SNOW DEPTH: 4′8″ (DRIFTS TO 20′)

FORECAST: SNOW ENDING TONIGHT,
CLEARING AND COLDER

After a brief conversation with the Secretary of Defense, the President announced to the National Security Council, "All actions proposed earlier on the assumption of Soviet responsibility have now been suspended. Admiral Clayton Greer, Commander in Chief of U.S. Atlantic forces, has changed the orders for our attack group from full-alert to second-level standby status." He sighed, loosening his blue-and-gray-striped tie. "Men need not be scrambling into Minuteman silos in Montana tonight." The moaning wind outside the Cabinet Room rose in pitch. The President looked down at Vice President Lindemann on his immediate right. "That might not be a bad place to hide."

Again he spoke to the Council. "We will now turn to the critical question of what can be done to terminate this blizzard." He beckoned to Paul, who was waiting at the side of the room next to Joni Dubin. "Dr. Garfield."

Even before Paul reached the head of the table, the Secretary of Defense addressed him. "Your explanation of Project Low Blow was very lucidly presented, but I'm having difficulty getting a fix on the rationale. It just doesn't make sense to me." The Secretary sucked on his pipe. "Why on earth would any American want to make such a test near our coastline where it would constitute a great potential danger?"

"I agree that it doesn't make sense," Paul replied. "I hope that my earlier remarks made my feelings clear in that regard. But, knowing those who must have made the decisions, I don't find it surprising. To be fair, everyone involved in the project, at least during my tenure there, believed that we had control of the system.

"First of all, heat generation by the reactors was a simple turn-on, turn-off situation. And secondly, after our successful test in the Pacific, it looked as though we had close control of the degree of storm modification." He shrugged. "It wouldn't have made much sense at any time if that hadn't been the case. A combination of unexpected problems must have arisen. The reactor-control system almost certainly has malfunctioned. It's highly unlikely that the storm would have remained stationary and intensified to this degree otherwise."

"But why our coastline, and why a blizzard?" Secretary Norris persisted.

"For a long time," Paul explained, "there had been a plan to test a winter storm, to see if we could slow down or even stop a cold-season convection cell and then deepen it." He glanced at General Wilcox. "Crank it up. The military objective was to acquire the capability of neutralizing the coastal facilities of an enemy in middle to high latitudes during winter."

"It seems that *we* have become the enemy," the Secretary of State observed.

"That's why it doesn't make any sense, Charlie," snapped Secretary Norris.

"Please continue, Dr. Garfield." The President was impatient.

"In all likelihood, secrecy was a principal factor in site selection." Paul opened the second button of his shirt front and folded his sleeves back to the elbows. The shirt was beginning to smell of sweat. "The original plan was to test Project Low Blow in harmless waters within our sphere of political and military control, to avoid discovery by other governments—or at least minimize the probability. Hell, even a minor international incident could have killed the project."

"Pity it didn't," lamented Mrs. Lindemann.

"Whether we had been trying to hide our experiments from the Soviets for treaty reasons or not, we clearly would have been for military purposes." Paul turned up his palms. "The great irony now, of course, is that the Russians probably discovered this test before any of us knew about it."

"My guess is that the reactors went down last spring—under the cover of those scuttled ships that stirred up so much controversy. I'm sure the publicity wasn't anticipated. It must have attracted the attention of the Soviets and led to their flurry of activity early last summer. They were probably there to check out what we were up to." Paul lit a cigarette. "As you know, they've got a stationary satellite due south of the site and six others crisscrossing it every twenty-four hours. You can be sure that they're aware of what's going on. They could probably nail us for violating treaty articles."

"That explains their U.N. gambit," commented Secretary Kroner. Vincent Satin frowned and blew his nose.

"If what you say is true," advanced General Wilcox, "then locating the test in our waters for increased security didn't do a damn bit of good. Backfired, to say the least. I could've thought of safer places than off our East Coast."

"Yes, but aside from reducing the chances of detection, the site was undoubtedly chosen to meet test requirements and, again, without consideration of risk. Not from the storm, anyway. Technically, the location is ideal," Paul continued. "It coincides with the center of an imaginary circle whose perimeter follows the arc of coastline between Cape Hatteras and Cape Cod." He was pointing at a large map of North America which had been set up on an easel-like

212

stand. "The counterclockwise circulation throws moist marine air into a continental cold front along the coast." He gave a shrug. "Works like a charm."

"More like a curse," grumbled General Wilcox.

"I'm sure they intended to produce no more than a minor winter storm," Paul pointed out. "A perfect disguise and a meaningful test. But marked changes in natural conditions must have combined with control breakdown to produce a blizzard of such magnitude. From what little I know about the storm's evolution, I infer that it was a relatively weak low moving across the Carolinas, but that it began to slow down and intensify to an unusual degree by itself as soon as it moved out to sea. In conjunction, the cold front sliding southeastward toward it slowed dramatically after passing a line between Washington and Boston. The potential for a major coastal storm was developing rapidly anyway. With a little boost from human ignorance, the cyclone stopped and ran wild."

"Where's the HQ for Project Low Blow?" the President asked.

"It used to be hidden under a complex of buildings called the Naval Ship Research and Development Center up the Potomac just past the Beltway. I'm certain that hasn't changed. That's OPCON: Operations Control."

"Are the experiments controlled directly from there?" questioned the Chief Executive.

"No, through one or the other of two so-called oceanographic research vessels: *Narwhal* and *Manatee*."

"*Manatee?*" Secretary Norris repeated. "That's the mother ship for our abyssal bathyscaphe."

"That's the one," Paul assured him. "The sub-

213

mersible's name is *Nessie*. We used it for confirming reactor orientation. Many of you may remember *Nessie* from publicity about the salvaging of a Russian sub a few years ago. The CIA had a hand in that, too." Paul hadn't been able to resist suggesting the connection. The President glanced at Vincent Satin, who was examining his fingernails.

"Dr. Garfield, surely Project Low Blow has some sort of emergency plan to correct a malfunction," offered Albert Kaufman optimistically.

"We had none for our initial experiment in the Pacific," Paul confessed. "Except for backup control systems and exhaustive pre-run testing. If they do now, you can be sure it will be one designed to keep the secret buried."

"When ya drop, you'll be carryin' enough water to get you to twenty fathoms in a few seconds," shouted First Engineer Nordquist. He gripped a railing and shifted his weight in a continuing effort to maintain balance inside the gyrating U.S.S. *Manatee*.

Matthew Rodek was dressed in insulated white coveralls that resembled a spacesuit. He was trying to close the zipper on a pocket just below his right hip. "Yeah, I'll be ready. Just be sure the fuckin' doors are open. That's one gate I don't want to crash." In the central hold of the Navy's oceanographic research ship, two large hydraulic arms held a cradlelike structure above bomb-bay doors in the bottom of the hull. Clamped in the cradle was a yellow submersible shaped like an enormous lemon. A thick screw-in hatch secured by cables hung over a hole in its top.

Rodek was inspecting a six-foot steel sphere attached to the nose of the submersible. "I hope to hell

214

that *Narwhal* doesn't set this mother off before I can get back out of range." He looked up at Nordquist on the overhanging catwalk. "Is Smith still pissed?"

" 'Fraid so," the engineer replied. "Can't really blame him, Matt. I think he's a little seasick, which is humiliating enough. But, you know, he's been training in *Nessie* for eight months. He was the senior active commander—even though he had never taken her down on a real mission. You were retired and out of the way, so he figures he should still be in command. You'd feel the same way, you ornery bastard."

"Ah, shit!" Rodek flipped his hand, then let himself fall forward to grasp the ladder on the side of the submersible. "Rookies always want to be the Most Valuable Player. The old instant-stardom bullshit. They want to jump to the top instead of climbin' up rung by rung." He climbed the ladder. "There's no substitute for experience. Fuck 'em." The *Manatee* dropped heavily over a large wave. Rodek fell back five feet onto a lower platform. "Goddam son of a bitch!" He scrambled to his feet. "This reminds me of Typhoon Rose." Back on the ladder, "How long you figure till we're in range—ready to go down?"

"Less than an hour now."

"What I want to know," blurted an aroused Secretary of State, "is who is responsible for this gross criminality?"

"As far as I know," Paul Garfield responded, "Admiral Curtis Zimber originally authorized and pushed through Project Low Blow. He established SWIRL and obtained the funding—all in secret, of course. Since then, I understand he's taken increasingly dictatorial control of the operation."

"My God," gasped the President. "Lloyd and I had a meeting with him just yesterday about the drone-submarine budget."

"That jingoistic bastard." Secretary Kroner flipped his glasses down on the table.

"And he was a stickler for secrecy," Paul added. "I mean *absolute* secrecy. I always thought it was greatly overdone. It was as though national survival depended upon the security of our project and violations were a form of treason. Nobody outside ever knew exactly what we were doing. They should've had Zimber direct the Watergate coverup."

"The man must be insane," assessed the Secretary of State. "It was *his* actions that were treasonable."

"Maybe more so than you realize," interjected David Bradford.

"Now just what does that mean, Senator?" demanded General Wilcox as he turned in his chair.

"We have uncovered evidence that Admiral Zimber was passing classified information to the Nationalist Chinese in return for funds funneled through them by the CIA," Bradford disclosed. "And with healthy discounts for himself as well as middlemen over there." These latest charges triggered a new outbreak of excited chatter around the room. The atmosphere was prickly; tempers were short.

"That's unadulterated horseshit!" Vincent Satin was almost screaming.

"An hour ago, I would've said this whole story was horseshit, Satin," said the President. As he stood up, other talking subsided. "Right now, however, the Senator's allegations seem pretty damn plausible."

Joni Dubin and Paul were watching each other. He turned to the President in support of David Bradford.

"The Taiwan government could well have a strategic interest in Low Blow. The East China Sea off the mainland is roughly comparable in geographic setting to the present storm site."

"Would Zimber be at the project headquarters?" the President asked abruptly.

"I doubt it," Paul replied. "He always avoided direct contact. He's probably at the Pentagon—or out of the country."

"Wilson," said the President to his advisor, "find Zimber and get him here immediately. I'll speak to him on the phone myself if necessary. And make damn sure a snow vehicle or Metro train is available so there can be no excuses about lack of transportation." The President's lips pressed tightly together; he was angry. Keithley-Smythe promptly departed as Herbert Salisbury approached the Chief Executive. He was clutching a notebook.

"Mr. President," said Salisbury, "Dan needs to see you as soon as possible. The press corps is raising hell. First it was the Metro shooting, and now the Russians have announced their U.N. move."

"Damn. Did they release any details?"

"Fortunately not. Just about the same wording as Kroner's statement to the Council. But you can imagine what kind of pressure is building."

"I can't see Dan now. We're just about to get to grips with this. He'll have to stall till we have a plan in motion. Play down the U.N. thing."

"Yes, sir. While you've got a minute, there are a couple of other items."

"What?" The President leaned closer to hear above the room noise and the whinning wind outside.

"We're getting some serious leaks and flooding because of snowdrifts building against the White House, especially here in the West Wing. Some of the staff think you should consider Operation Exodus before the blizzard gets any worse."

"We sure as hell couldn't fly out now," returned the Chief Executive.

"No, but the Commander submarine is ready to take us south to a carrier in calm water. Then we would fly by helicopter to an air base out of the storm zone and transfer to the 747."

"Well, confirm the logistics. I'll decide later. Anything else?"

"A number of scientists have asked to see you and Albert Kaufman. A Dr. Uriah from the National Academy of Sciences is waiting across the street in the Office of Science and Tech. They say it's urgent."

"Put the scientists off and have Albert talk to Uriah. There's no way . . . wait, here comes Wilson."

Wilson Keithley-Smythe walked directly to the President. "Zimber's in the Pentagon but is 'indisposed,'" he reported. "I talked to somebody named Popowski. He assured me that he would relay your orders to Admiral Zimber. A Metro car has been dispatched to pick them up."

"Good. Maybe we're starting to get someplace." The President turned to Paul Garfield. "Do you know this Popowski?"

"He's a civilian, a twenty-five-year Navy retiree. His title in ONR was Project Coordinator, but effectively he's been Zimber's chief administrative assistant."

"Admiral?" Walter Popowski leaned into Curtis Zimber's darkened Pentagon office. He waited motionless, holding the door ajar for several seconds. He had expected the Admiral to have fallen asleep again—he had been drinking heavily—but the couch was empty. "Admiral?" he repeated. "Train's here." Popowski was talking as though he knew that someone was listening, trying to reassure himself that Zimber was there. "Judgment Day," he called. Still no reply. Only the disquieting buzz of intense silence. The bathroom light was on.

Popowski entered the office and closed the door. "You ready, Admiral?" Now he was shouting. He turned on the light and walked quickly across to the bathroom door. The Admiral had dropped his razor on the white tile floor. Beyond it lay a dark-red pool of thickening blood. As Popowski inched forward, the upper body came into view. Admiral Curtis Jackson Zimber had sliced open his throat just below the larynx with his father's straight-edged razor.

21

〰〰〰〰〰〰〰〰〰〰〰〰〰〰〰〰〰〰〰〰〰〰

WASHINGTON NATIONAL AIRPORT:
   10:00 PM, FRIDAY, DECEMBER 22

TEMPERATURE: 23°F

BAROMETER: 28.59″ (FALLING)

WIND: NE 45–70 MPH

SNOW DEPTH: 4′10″ (DRIFTS TO 23′)

FORECAST: SNOW ENDING TONIGHT,
   CLEARING AND COLDER

"Poor bastard looks like he's back from the dead," whispered the Chairman of the Joint Chiefs to CIA Director Satin. General Wilcox was peering sideways at the tired figure near the head of the table. Like his wrinkled suit, Walter Popowski looked limp and gray. His shirt was open, his tie stuffed into his coat pocket. He was perspiring and in need of a shave.

"Get to the point," prodded the President. "Exactly what is this emergency plan?"

Popowski was trembling. He kept clutching his Adam's apple. He hadn't mustered the courage to reveal Curtis Zimber's suicide; he had reported only that the Admiral was ill. "We're going to try . . . we're going to stop the reactors." His speech came in bursts, occasionally with stuttering.

"That's wonderful," sniped Secretary Norris. "But how? We all agree that they should be stopped." He glanced around the room.

It was somewhat less crowded now; several aides had been sent on missions, and two of the visiting Congressional leaders were temporarily away. The atmosphere of the meeting was superficially more informal. White House stewards had served tea and coffee during the wait for Popowski's arrival. Cups and saucers and napkins lay scattered on the table, coats hung on the back of chairs, shirt collars were open with ties loosened. But the undercurrent was one of tension and impatience. Against the background sounds of gusting wind and vibrating glass, the prolonged pressure was beginning to tell.

"*N-N-N-Nessie*'s going down to place a charge. Commanders Rodek and Smith are piloting."

"You mean they're going to blow up the reactors?" shouted Paul incredulously.

"That is c-c-c-correct."

"That is also crazy!" Paul looked at the President, then around the table to Albert Kaufman. "That would release their radioactive wastes—eventually into the Gulf Stream." He swept his arm in a broad arc. "It would poison the entire North Atlantic. The *entire* North Atlantic!"

Popowski sighed tremulously. "Destroy the evidence. That was Zimber's decision. That is the policy." Jerkily, he glanced from one face to another, but didn't seem to find what he was looking for.

"Fortunately, destroying those reactors is much easier said than done." Paul seemed to have relaxed a little. "It would take massive charges. They're virtually impregnable." He stared at Popowski but could not fix the other's attention. The beleaguered witness was gazing up at the closer of the Cabinet Room's two chandeliers. His expression was blank. "What kind of charges?" Garfield demanded.

At length, Popowski muttered, "Nuclear mine."

"What?" shouted the President.

"Oh, my God," gasped Paul. The President rose to his feet.

Manatee was pitching wildly in waves driven by hurricane-force winds. "The Captain'll wait until we fall into a broad trough, then drop you during the lull," yelled Mr. Nordquist.

Rodek compressed his lips, gave a thumbs-up sign, and grabbed the ladder railing. Turning to Duncan Smith, he asked, "Worried?"

"No, why should I be? Are you?"

"A little. I'm leery of this damn mine. The pressures down there might set the thing off before we can get away."

"Not possible," Smith snapped. "It can only be activated by radio signal."

Rodek ushered him up the ladder. "You go on in

first. Smarts before wisdom." Smith was studiously serious and didn't reply. In a moment he dropped out of sight through the hatchway. As Rodek started up, the *Manatee* crashed over a wave crest and threw him hard against the submersible's hull. He regained his footing and started climbing toward the hatch. "Take 'er easy, *Nessie*. Here comes Papa."

"*Narwhal* has orders to set off the mine by radio signal as soon as they get down there," Popowski revealed.

"You mean, after *Nessie* has moved back out of range," Paul corrected.

Popowski shook his head. "No."

"What?"

" 'Destroy the evidence' was Zimber's plan," the harried witness repeated. "Delta code."

"Well, we're not married to that goddam plan," responded Secretary Norris.

"Delta code!" Paul exclaimed. " 'Destroy the evidence,' he says. Never mind the ocean . . . or the two men in the sub!" He smeared his cigarette in the ash tray.

"Have they started down yet?" asked the President.

"Not as of half an hour ago," Popowski answered, "but they're getting close."

"Even if they have begun their dive, we'll order them back up," stated the Chief Executive.

"I'm afraid that wouldn't be possible, sir." Popowski glanced nervously at the President.

"And why not?"

Walter Popowski pulled a wrinkled white handkerchief from his right hip pocket and wiped his face.

"Starting with the Cuban experiment, Zimber has run *Nessie* silent on these missions."

"Please explain that," the President demanded.

"She's got no receiver and only a short-range beeper transmitter for location purposes. That's how *Narwhal* tracks her—along with sonar, of course." Popowski expelled a deep sigh. "The Admiral didn't want to risk interception."

Looking into Paul Garfield's eyes, the President slowly shook his head. "I wouldn't have believed it. Absolutely unfathomable."

At that moment, the screw-in hatch on top of the abyssal bathyscaphe was being rotated by the metallic talons of a mechanical arm. In the wheelhouse of the plunging *Manatee*, Mr. Nordquist reported to the Captain, "Ready to drop in five minutes." Both men braced themselves against another fall. The Captain bumped the bulkhead.

"Is Berger on the radio?" the Captain asked his First Mate, who was standing in the entranceway.

"Yes. Want me to pass the word?"

"No, I need to talk to him myself." The Captain launched himself in the direction of the radio shack.

A few seconds later he heard Arnold Berger's voice through a barrage of static. "Yes, Captain. I'm listening."

"Berger, we're about ready to lay our egg. Any final instructions for Rodek and Smith?"

There was another burst of noise from the speaker. "No, Captain. No changes. Better stick to the emergency orders."

"All of them?"

"You can read as well as I can," came the quick reply. "Delta code."

The President walked over to Defense Secretary Norris. "Lloyd, will you transmit the order to *Manatee* not to release that submersible? There's got to be a better way than this."

"Of course, Mr. President." Norris stood up.

The Chief Executive turned back to Popowski. "All right, now get your operations room on the line for the Secretary of Defense."

"Yes, sir," in a whisper. Secretary Norris followed Popowski and Herbert Salisbury out of the room.

Paul Garfield and Albert Kaufman immediately approaced the President. Dr. Kaufman spoke first. "I pray to God we're in time, Mr. President. A nuclear explosion of sufficient magnitude to destroy those reactors could have disastrous side effects in addition to releasing radioactive waste and alarming the Soviets."

"That's right, sir," Paul elaborated. "It might trigger submarine landslides off the continental slope and generate seismic sea waves—'tidal' waves."

"My God." The President paused. "Kroner's right. Zimber *must* be insane. How could he possible rationalize this—let alone cover it up?"

"He'd probably claim it was an accident," Paul offered. "Oh, Mr. President. While we have OPCON on the line, perhaps you should request that a couple of their people come down here to help us on contingency planning. Arnold Berger is probably in charge there now."

The President nodded solemnly. "Will you come

with me, Garfield?" The two walked rapidly toward the door.

The sealed lower half of *Manatee*'s central hold had been filled with water. *Nessie* lay in her massive steel cradle; her underside resembled the closed jaws of a giant power shovel. The cradle was descending toward the bomb-bay doors in *Manatee*'s hull. When it had approached within a few feet of them, the doors parted and began to whir-r-r out into the swirling sea beneath the *Manatee*.

On the bridge, the Captain announced, "After the next big crest, we'll straighten out and drop her." As the bow began to rise, the First Mate rushed in from the radio shack waving a piece of paper.

Below in the hold, the bomb-bay doors were wide open. Then slowly they started to close.

22

~~~~~~

WASHINGTON NATIONAL AIRPORT:
    11:00 PM, FRIDAY, DECEMBER 22

TEMPERATURE: 23°F

BAROMETER: 28.56″ (FALLING)

WIND: NE 45–75 MPH

SNOW DEPTH: 5′ (DRIFTS TO 25′)

FORECAST: SNOW ENDING TONIGHT,
    CLEARING AND COLD

Everyone in the Cabinet Room was tired. The eyes of
those seated around the large table were fixed on a
variety of visual resting places: the portraits, the windows, the map of North America, or on pencils tap-

ping yellow legal pads. The voice of Arnold Berger was coming from a speaker-phone wired into the room's sound system. Larger wall speakers on order had not arrived yet.

"I'm in SWIRL OpCon now. We got through to *Manatee* in time to stop the submersible's dive. *Nessie* is still in her hold, and *Manatee* is moving directly away from the storm center at all possible speed back toward the eastern tip of Long Island." This news had been relayed moments earlier by one of Berger's colleagues, so it came as no surprise or cause for rejoicing. Berger had been outside the Operations Control room at the time. After his initial announcement, there was a pause; background talking could be heard coming over the speaker-phone.

During the interruption in Berger's report, Paul Garfield leaned over to Joni Dubin. "Just listen to him. Now that he has no choice, he'll be the self-righteous opportunist—ready to be a hero. The man can't be trusted."

Arnold Berger started again. Some of his remarks apparently had not been transmitted, because he seemed to be in the midst of a new topic: "We could close all Soviet ports in the future—but we couldn't risk even the remote possibility of their interpretation of our experiment as an act of aggression now." Paul eyed the Secretary of State, who turned up his palm and shrugged as Berger continued. "So, we decided to test winter-storm enhancement in the northwest Atlantic off our own coast for a very brief, controlled period." Berger had now gained the attention of everybody.

He elaborated. "Twelve hours would give us the data we needed and in a location where we would have optimum opportunity for control and measurement. Moreover, it would create no more difficulties than occur naturally almost every year."

"Hah!" said Secretary Norris.

Paul Garfield was listening with great interest to the words of his old enemy and former colleague. "What has happened is that we have been unable—for the first time—to turn the reactors off."

"We know that, for Christ's sakes," shouted General Wilcox.

Berger could hear what was said in the Cabinet Room, but he did not respond to the General. "In spite of numerous successful tests subsequent to the reactor's placement last spring, it does not now acknowledge or obey radio commands."

The President addressed a two-way speaker. "Berger, what do you think has happened?"

"Perhaps the antennae were damaged during placement. But that would mean that the system was behaving inconsistently, because it responded normally in trial runs before initiation of the actual storm experiment." Berger apparently was speaking to someone else; muffled talking could be heard in the background.

Then he continued, "We are monitoring abnormally high heat values in the electronic capsules. Perhaps there was some sort of cumulative heat damage to the circuitry. Alternatively," Berger coughed a couple of times, "excuse me, there is, of course, some possibility of outside interference."

"Here we go again," commented the President. "What do you mean by that?"

"Well, I guess you'd have to call it 'sabotage.' Last spring and summer, we were afraid that the Soviets were on to us. You know, at the time of the May Day satellite and ship incident. It's conceivable that they have taken advantage of the situation."

The Secretary of Defense pursued the point. "So they *are* responsible after all!"

"Who is speaking now?"

"Secretary of Defense Lloyd Norris."

"Thank you, sir. You all realize that I am unfamiliar with your voices, so it would make it easier for me if you would identify yourselves when you ask questions. Now, we have no evidence of Russian interference. It's just wild speculation. The responsibility is a terrible one to assume, but it's probably ours. My judgment is that the problem with the system is more likely to be internal."

The Chairman of the Joint Chiefs pulled a well-chewed cigar from his mouth and piped up, "I don't follow. Why couldn't those bastards have dropped something down there to screw up our controls? They could be operating it from their ships or Cosmos satellites."

"Who was that?"

"General Wilcox."

"Well, General, as I said, that is possible. But we have no evidence to support such an allegation. We should have been able to see the actual placement electronically."

"Wilcox again: Maybe their gadget was too small. And that's just the point," he shouted. "If they could screw up our controls, they could sure as hell screen our detection systems some way or other. Neutralization of weapons-detection systems is a damned advanced technology."

"Yes, sir. I know that."

"Arnold, this is Paul Garfield. What about short-range transmission? Say, put a contact transmitter on the master reactor? It might work even if the antenna system is damaged."

"Yes, we've talked about that. But Zimber thought it was too uncertain. He wanted to destruct. We had an alternative troubleshooting plan that involved fitting *Nessie*'s nose with a contact transmitter."

The President straightened up. "This is the President. Can that plan be put into effect immediately?"

"Yes, sir, but *Manatee* would have to return to New London. We have the encased transmitter in storage there. It would be fitted with an electromagnetic attachment coupling and one of the collars for *Nessie*'s nose."

"Secretary of Defense Norris speaking. How would you get it there? I thought that *Manatee* almost broke up in those hurricane waves."

"A submarine—probably in the Poseidon class—would have to be readied to tow *Nessie* below the storm center at fifty fathoms. If the reactors could not be stopped, the Poseidon would have to destroy them with nuclear depth charges."

"This is the President again. Dr. Garfield has told us that destroying the reactors in that way might release very dangerous radioactive wastes into the Gulf Stream. Could that be avoided?"

"Not entirely, Mr. President. I guess you'd have to say that it would constitute the lesser of two evils."

"Arnold, Paul again. I don't think the towing plan is feasible. The submersible pilots—even one man—wouldn't have enough oxygen for that long a time."

"That's right. Of course, the plan didn't anticipate

rough seas over such a large area. It was to have been a relatively short tow."

"Could *Nessie* be mounted on the sub's deck?"

"Maybe. We're working on that now."

"Secretary of State speaking. I have been thinking about all of these remarks, and I want to go on record as being in agreement with Dr. Berger's interpretation of the possible causes of this catastrophe. I do not believe that the Soviet Union would have risked involvement in such a foolish adventure," turning toward the Secretary of Defense and the Chairman of the Joint Chiefs, "such as you gentlemen have alleged."

The President stood up. "I suggest that the alternate emergency plan just outlined by Dr. Berger be initiated immediately." The President looked up toward the ceiling. "Dr. Berger?"

"Yes, Mr. President?"

"Can you have an updated report on the progress of this plan ready for our meeting at nine o'clock tomorrow morning?"

"Yes, sir."

"And will you be prepared to come down here yourself?"

"Yes, sir."

"Good. You can keep in touch with everything through our Situation Room. Now," the President cleared his throat, "the Council stands adjourned until nine A.M." It was a few minutes before midnight.

"Hang on! Hang on! I'll lift you up." Paul struggled to gain more secure footing as he resisted Joni's pull on his arm. Her feet were pedaling in the air, brushing rock dust from the face of the cliff be-

232

low. He lodged his heel against the back of the narrow ledge and began to lift her with painful slowness. His heel slipped! Pine needles? Moss? He was falling forward. He would plunge over the edge, pulled downward by the sinking weight of his mate—unless he let go. And in pure reflex, he did. He heard her screaming even after she had dropped so far as to shrink into invisibility. He hadn't noticed, he didn't remember that the rock pile they had climbed was so high. It must be miles to the bottom.

He was jerking and grasping on the couch. "Joni. Joni," he called.

"I'm here. What is it?" She lay down next to him and they hugged each other.

"I . . . I had a dream," he explained meekly. She kissed him gently in a way that she hadn't done for a long time. "Are you back?" he asked.

"Yes, I'm back." She smiled. The wall clock in Senator Bradford's outer office showed that it was 1:45 in the morning.

"Where's David?" Paul wondered.

"He's inside, working on his evidence. He's where you used to be. And you . . . you're where you should have been."

"What's changed?" He couldn't believe it.

"Everything. I've learned a lot about you in the past two days. And about David. And myself. Your spirit is free now, but his isn't. I've gotten to know a new person, and I'm so glad it's you." They gazed at each other in the darkness, not hearing the wind.

23

〜〜〜〜〜〜〜〜〜〜〜〜〜〜〜〜〜〜〜〜〜〜〜〜

WASHINGTON NATIONAL AIRPORT:
9:00 AM, SATURDAY, DECEMBER 23

TEMPERATURE: 22°F

BAROMETER: 28.34″ (FALLING)

WIND: NE 50–85 MPH

SNOW DEPTH: 8′4″ (DRIFTS TO 6 STORIES)

FORECAST: SNOW ENDING THIS MORNING,
CLEARING AND COLD

Jane Conroy looked like hell. Her eyes were red and circled, her hair dirty and disheveled. She turned up the volume on her television set and sat down on a footstool to sip coffee and listen to the news, which was now being broadcast continuously.

". . . level of snow depth is impossible to determine. This white hurricane has blown the snow into great undulating dunelike mounds. Some drifts are as much as four stories high, burying many small buildings." The newscaster looked almost as bad as Jane. His shirt was open and sweat-stained, his tie dangling far below his belt. "The storm itself has further intensified into a full-blown hurricane with winds up to one hundred and forty miles per hour near its center and barometric pressure down nearly to twenty-eight inches. Folks," he let his handful of papers flop down against his thigh, "I just don't know what to tell you. You can't see anything, you can't go anywhere. It's even too deep for King Kong. In New York, Manhattan's invisible skyline must be like a forest of spruce trees sticking out of a mountain snowbank."

Jane lit a cigarette. No, you can't see anything. You can't go anywhere. You can't do anything. Can't use the phone. She took a long drag and snorted smoke out through her nostrils. Jane hadn't been able to sleep much. Restless and worrying. What had happened to John? And what had happened to Paul? She looked back at the television screen.

". . . power and telephone failures are now commonplace. There is much overheating and flooding, and serious inconvenience due to shortages of supplies, which have run out or are running out in many localities. Weakly supported roofs have been collapsing under the weight of accumulated snow and enormous drifts advancing over them." The man referred to his notes. Jane felt chilly and wrapped a blanket around her shoulders. "Especially dangerous are supermarkets, other large shopping-center buildings, bowling alleys, and warehouses. Unfortunately," he looked up, "some of these buildings have been serving as shelters for the stranded.

"Thousands of reports of local emergencies have been pouring in. But because of the almost total communications and transportation paralysis in the blizzard zone, relief efforts are proving ineffective. Federalization and coordination of all governmental agencies as authorized under the National Emergency declaration and organized by the newly created Blizzard Relief Council seem to have made little difference.

"In New York City, the last workable means of public transportation has finally become inoperative. Subways," nodding at the camera, "are just plain chaos. Thousands upon thousands of people are living under the city there: stranded, cold, hungry, and—worse—defenseless. Trains had to be halted. A number of people have been run over because of crowding; others have been electrocuted. Trains have actually been derailed. Drivers could not be relieved, so became exhausted." The newsman frowned. "Some have been beaten, one reportedly killed. There simply was no way for them to maintain control of their trains. We're talking about mob rule, ladies and gentlemen. It's really getting vicious down there." He started shaking his head. "This is no mild emergency any more. No more parties. This is a disaster," spoken deliberately for emphasis. "We are living with terror."

Jane got up and walked out to the kitchen to pour another cup of coffee. She noticed water stains along the edge of the kitchen ceiling. Must be from the high humidity. She returned to the television set.

". . . armed gangs are terrorizing the helpless where no police protection is present. In their efforts to offset the spreading anarchy, some policemen have been killed, others disarmed and abused. The fascists among us are emerging," Jane puckered out a neat stream of smoke, "feeding on disorder as they have throughout history." He glanced up from his paper. "Hopefully, federalized National Guard troops now en route—and don't ask me how—to the city and within the city will be able to help in re-establishing law and order. Unfortunately, thus far, very few troops have actually arrived where needed most.

"A little later in this broadcast, we will review for you the special regulations which have come into effect as a result of the National Emergency. Also, we will read a selection of the emergency suggestions and recommendations which have been issued by various governmental agencies at the local, state, and national levels, now all under federal jurisdiction. So, please stay tuned for this forthcoming emergency information. It is of vital importance—literally—to all of us."

Jane blew a plume of smoke toward the ceiling and watched it disturb a layer that had stratified across the room. Then she noticed a fringe of water stain along the top of the wall between the dining room and the kitchen. She couldn't remember that much condensation ever before.

"The growing network of improvised tunnels in and under the snow is very dangerous for several reasons. First, there is the obvious threat of collapse, burial, and suffocation by mini-avalanches, cave-ins, and the like. More dangerous than the snow, however, are the people. Obviously, law enforcement in such tunnel systems is next to impossible. In many localities, local gangs of looters have established territories. There are reports of deadly inter-gang guerrilla warfare." He set his jaw. "It's kill or be killed.

"This works a double hardship on those persons who must venture outside in search of supplies or assistance. It is certainly safer to stay home." He waved toward a map. "Similar situations exist throughout the disaster area. Incidentally," again he dropped his pages to his side, "the storm is now officially being referred to as 'The Great American Blizzard,' or simply, 'The Blizzard.'

"The magnitude of the disaster is creating ever greater pressures on those who are attempting to relieve the suffering and bring an end to this greatest snowstorm in history. At this very hour, the National Security Council is again meeting in emergency session. There has as yet been no opportunity for questions by members of the White House press corps, although White House Press Secretary Dan Simon promised late last night to meet with reporters some time today. Thus far, only two brief, general announcements regarding the NSC meetings have been released by the White House. However, rumors are multiplying. The most widely accepted is that the storm is not natural, but is a result of weather warfare being waged either by the Soviet Union or by the People's Republic of China. The Russians' so-called May Day Cosmos satellite seems to be the most popular villain. The second choice is damage allegedly done to the earth's ozone layer by supersonic aircraft." Jane was watching drops of water fall from the dining-room ceiling to the floor.

"Lending some credence to suspicions of the hand of man in this so-called natural disaster is the presence at the White House of a number of scientists who have in the past been associated with weather-modification research or are regarded as leading authorities on applied meterorology. Among those who have been seen—" His notes fluttered to the floor. "Oops! Damn." He stooped to retrieve them, then straightened up. "Excuse me, ladies and gentlemen.

"Now," again referring to his notes, "among those scientists who have been seen entering the White House are Professor Harold Uriah, Nobel Laureate and President of the National Academy of Sciences, and Dr. Paul Garfield, formerly of NASA and the Office of Naval Research." Jane's hands were trembling. She spilled hot coffee into her saucer. So he's here. How did he ever manage that? She stood up and breathed a deep sigh. She felt comforted just knowing that Paul had come down. Perhaps there was still a chance of finding John. Her eyes moistened; a tear crept down her cheek.

Water was dripping rapidly from the dining-room ceiling. At once she realized that there was far too much for condensation. Maybe a pipe had broken. There must be flooding upstairs. She moved quickly into the hallway and bounded upward in her bathrobe two steps at a time. The guest room was over the dining-room and kitchen. Must be a leak in its bathroom. She felt a chill: cold air.

She opened the door into a burst of frigid air and snow; the window had blown in. Building over the bed and across the floor was a snowdrift four feet high. She stood there shivering and watched in disbelief as the white mass advanced, inch by inch. The drift was growing. Moving as if by will.

24

≈≈≈≈≈≈≈≈≈≈≈≈≈≈≈≈≈≈≈≈≈≈≈≈≈≈≈≈≈≈≈≈≈≈≈≈≈≈≈

**WASHINGTON NATIONAL AIRPORT:
9:00 AM, SATURDAY, DECEMBER 23**

TEMPERATURE: 22°F

BAROMETER: 28.34″ (FALLING)

WIND: NE 50–85 MPH

SNOW DEPTH: 8′4″ (DRIFTS TO 6 STORIES)

**FORECAST: SNOW ENDING THIS MORNING,
CLEARING AND COLD**

The Cabinet Room was filled to capacity. All chairs around the long table were occupied, as were those lining the walls. Sitting at the table were the members of the National Security Council, the newly formed Blizzard Relief Council, and several agency representatives and military personnel. As during the long meeting the night before, seated around the sides of the room were the leaders of Congress, invited witnesses and experts, and others involved in the crisis, including Senator Bradford, Paul Garfield, and Joni Dubin.

The Chief of Naval Operations was speaking. "The Navy's abyssal bathyscaphe . . ."

Paul whispered to Joni, "He's the only person I know who refuses to use the name 'Nessie.' He probably doesn't believe in the Loch Ness monster."

". . . being mounted on the deck of the Poseidon submarine *Leopard Shark*. As I understand was discussed here last night, the earlier plan of towing the submersible proved impracticable because the pilot or pilots would have had to remain inside the abyssal bathyscaphe for the entire journey, and there was insufficient oxygen for the time required."

"Ah, Admiral . . ."

"Yes, sir, Mr. President."

"As you mentioned, we have covered this already. Could you hurry ahead and fill us in on the update?"

"Yes," muttered the Secretary of Defense. "Let's get down to the nitty-gritty."

"Of course, gentlemen. You'll have that input very shortly. I did prepare a brief outline to give an overview." He cleared his throat and continued more loudly. "Moreover, the Navy's abyssal bathyscaphe was not able to carry sufficient fuel for the return to the surface outside the region of hurricane-force winds, thereby making safe recovery very difficult, if not impossible. Now," continued the Chief, "the plan is for *Leopard Shark* to cruise under the storm at a depth of fifty fathoms with the Navy's abyssal bathyscaphe mounted on her deck, then to surface in the eye of this winter hurricane.

"The Navy's research vessel *Narwhal* has remained in the eye—in truth, it's trapped there—continually monitoring meteorological and oceanographic variables and transmitting them to us." He was reading from his notes. "Waves are less than five feet in the eye, winds steady at four knots."

"Absolutely incredible!" exclaimed General Wilcox. "I find that astounding—it *is* a hurricane. Or a hurricane-blizzard, blizzard-hurricane."

"Please continue, Admiral," requested the President.

"Once on the surface, Commanders Rodek and Smith will board the abyssal bathyscaphe, be lowered by deck crane into the water, and dive to the bottom. After attaching the contact transmitter and issuing commands to cease controlled fission, the Navy's abyssal bathyscaphe will resurface in the eye to be picked up again by *Leopard Shark*. If the mission is unsuccessful, *Leopard Shark* is prepared to destroy the reactor with nuclear depth charges."

"Is *Nessie* being re-equipped with its original radio receiving and transmitting equipment?" asked Paul.

"Yes. No more deaf-and-dumb runs." The Chief paused, then asked, "Are there any other questions?"

After a moment of murmuring, the President inquired, "Are you through, Sam?"

"I am. Unless you'd like me to go into further detail about the characteristics of the Navy's abyssal bathyscaphe?"

"No, but can you tell us how soon *Leopard Shark* is expected to depart New London with *Nessie* aboard and when you anticipate their arrival below the eye?"

"Should leave any minute, arrive in twenty-four hours."

"And how long to the bottom?" questioned the Secretary of Transportation.

"Less than an hour."

"Thank you, Sam," said the President.

The next report was presented by Malcolm White, Director of the Federal Disaster Assistance Administration, who summarized current conditions. "Supply by sea and distribution by snow vehicles are the only ways we have of tackling the transportation problem. The convoy of transport and landing craft is now working its way up the Intracoastal Waterway but is having considerable difficulty because of essentially zero visibility; snow is being blown horizontally by hurricane winds. It is so thick that if it were accumulating vertically, I am told, its depth would increase—as it apparently had been—by two inches every hour. A rate of four feet per day!"

"Mother of God," whispered the Speaker of the House of Representatives.

"The blizzard zone is quite literally immobilized. Utilities are failing. People are now dying of exposure by the thousands. Supplies of all kinds are running out. And, in spite of the plethora of emergency plans and orders which have been adopted at every level of government, the sad fact is that there is hardly anything we can do to relieve most of the suffering, whether merely matters of inconvenience or of life and death.

"Most of the rest of the country—indeed, most of the world—is relatively unaffected. Everybody wants to help," he sighed, "but they can't. They can't get in." The Director's comments were having a visibly depressing influence.

"The intracoastal convoy," he went on, "is bringing hundreds of tread vehicles plus thousands of tons of supplies. The basics: food, fuel, and medical stores. But as long as the blizzard continues at the present level of intensity, this sea lift will amount to little more than a token insofar as overall effectiveness is concerned."

In the face of these disturbing facts, feelings of helplessness, hopelessness, even panic were not far below the surface around the Cabinet Room. The President flipped a pencil down on his pad in frustration, then addressed a question to the Chief of Naval Operations. "Sam, every minute of this blizzard means death to some of our citizens. Is there no way to accelerate the submarine mission?"

"Twenty-four hours is minimum," the Chief replied.

The Secretary of State lurched to his feet and put his hands on his hips. "How could this have happened? We are *totally* unprepared. This is like some sort of crazy nightmare! Who could have dreamed of such a catastrophe? Who can believe that we actually have forty feet of snow drifting over our heads?" He threw his arms out in a shrug of frustration and let them flop to his sides. Then he hurried out of the room.

"Crisis, crisis, crisis. I was countin' on a couple more hours of sack time," complained Matthew Rodek, pulling on a thermal undershirt.

"They're getting new maximum-speed orders

directly from the White House every hour on the hour," replied Lieutenant Commander Duncan Smith. "They must have *Nessie* mounted and ready to go. I'm anxious to see how fast they'll push *Leopard Shark* in a real emergency. I'll guess forty knots," as he pulled off his pajama top.

"Hey, Smith, you oughta do some weightliftin' or somethin'—lookin' kinda puny." Rodek yawned. "You're right about the speed; they could push her that fast, all right, but I don't think they'll dare with that jerry-rigged mount for *Nessie* on deck."

In five minutes Rodek and Smith were fully suited and waiting to board *Leopard Shark*. The huge submarine lay in a calm chute of water between rubber-lined concrete piers in a gigantic enclosed dock: a great hangarlike structure at the Navy's submarine center off the New London, Connecticut. Rodek had just inspected *Nessie*: her mountings; the plug-shaped, steel-encased contact transmitter on her nose collar; and the derrick system that would transfer her from the deck into the Atlantic. He spat into the water and looked down at Smith, who was standing on the deck. "You know, that fuckin' Zimber was gonna blow us up?"

At that moment began a loud creaking; then a screaming, exploding crash and the roar of the wind. The roof was collapsing. Men were running along the piers. Great leaves of aluminized fiber glass peeled down from the ceiling, together with segments of steel superstructure. Through the tearing rent in the roof plummeted massive blocks of snow, small icebergs in swirling clouds of snow.

In a few minutes, only the roar of the snow-choked

wind continued. The roof at the rear of the hangar was gone, but the rest had held. The submarine was undamaged. "Jesus," whispered Rodek, visibly paled, "that goddam storm is tryin' to stop us."

25

~~~~~~

WASHINGTON NATIONAL AIRPORT:
8:00 PM, SATURDAY, DECEMBER 23

TEMPERATURE: 21°F

BAROMETER: 28.13″ (FALLING)

WIND: NE 60–90 MPH

SNOW DEPTH: 8′4″ (DRIFTS TO 6 STORIES)

FORECAST: SNOW ENDING TONIGHT,
CLEARING AND COLDER

The Blizzard was on exhibit in the Cabinet Room. A young Navy officer had just taped a six-foot-square satellite photograph of the storm to a display board. Holding a notebook, a grease pencil, and a ruler, he studied the print and his notes for a moment, then drew an X near the upper left-hand edge of the cloud spiral. Next, he ruled a straight line toward a small dark spot in its center: the eye. The President entered from his adjoining suite, accompanied by Defense Secretary Norris and Wilson Keithley-Smythe. As soon as the President sat down, the Chief of Naval Operations rose and walked over to the photograph. The time was 8:06.

"Tonight we have good news and bad news," the Chief began. Paul Garfield returned a faint smile from Joni Dubin. "The good news is that the termination mission narrowly avoided abort due to collapse of part of the submarine-pier roof in New London, and that *Leopard Shark* and *Nessie* got underway two hours earlier than we had originally expected. Moreover, they have just passed Block Island, so they're out of the Sound and in the open Atlantic." The Chief pointed to the X on the photograph.

"That didn't sound like very good news to me," droned Secretary Kroner.

"And the bad news, General?" prodded the President.

"The bad news is that, due to the temporary and fragile nature of the bathyscaphe mountings, *Leopard Shark* is unable to make more than ten knots submerged. The drag is too great at higher speeds—not enough strength."

"What about surface travel?" inquired Defense Secretary Norris.

"Much worse. Absolutely out of the question. The swell would break off the submersible in no time."

"So what, then, is your projected arrival time in the eye?" asked the President.

249

"Between eleven hundred and twelve hundred hours tomorrow." He moved his finger along the line to the dark spot on the satellite photograph. This prediction was greeted by grumbles of frustration.

Dr. André Geler, Director of NOAA, rose next to present a brief report. "I trust that you have all had an opportunity to examine the handouts summarizing the latest storm-emergency data. Of greatest importance are those from *Narwhal* and our squadron of hurricane-hunter planes." He sighed. "I regret to say that the situation has deteriorated further. The storm continues to intensify and still shows no sign of moving off. The goddam thing is gigantic."

Subsequent summaries and evaluations of emergency measures were no more sanguine. Perhaps for this reason, they were shorter than before. Also, available information was less complete. Secretary Kroner expressed the helplessness felt by most of those present when he observed, "Complete mobilization of all available resources has had about as much effect as trying to stop the tides."

The President announced a short break, and a platoon of White House stewards entered to serve coffee. During this intermission, an extraordinarily large man was ushered into the room by Herbert Salisbury. They were accompanied by Albert Kaufman and Paul Garfield. The newcomer must have stood six feet six and weighed close to three hundred pounds. Thick white hair curled against the collar of his black pin-striped suitcoat. Upon the departure of the coffee servers, the President introduced the imposing gentleman.

"Since yesterday afternoon, we have received an increasing number of requests from members of the scientific community to appear before the Council. Their purpose is to explain a variety of concerns which they feel are of critical importance to the national security. As you will recall, at this morning's meeting, we agreed to invite their representative here tonight." The President turned and nodded to the guest. "Dr. Harold Uriah, President of the National Academy of Sciences, we are honored by your presence."

Professor Uriah moved to the head of the table. He carefully examined his audience, smiling and acknowledging each person whose eyes he met. He was afforded full attention and respectful silence. A minister of hope to the hopeless. He began slowly in deep, resonant tones. "I thank you for this hearing. I have a number of ideas which I wish to express this evening, but I must apologize in advance for their failure of organization." He unbuttoned his jacket and looked down at the floor.

"I hold conflicting views concerning the desperate remedy of destroying the offending reactors." He looked up. "I am told that the dangers of radioactive contamination and of submarine landslides and seismic sea waves were earlier competently enunciated by Dr. Garfield. However, not presuming to play the role of devil's advocate, I feel compelled to relate other, perhaps even more ominous possibilities.

"Dire as the aforementioned consequences of a nuclear explosion might be, we can at least foresee and understand them. Their scope is neither unlimited nor entirely beyond our experience; therefore, we can survive them and attempt to offset them. But the Great Blizzard, the man-made monster under whose works we are now buried—*it* is an altogether different

251

matter." Professor Uriah turned to look at the satellite photograph.

"Here we are experimenting with the unknown, interfering with natural relationships we do not begin to comprehend. No one can predict what irreversible reactions might be catalyzed by the products of our ignorance, our blind conceit in the supremacy of man." Paul Garfield felt as though the professor were lecturing him alone.

"Now, let me be more explicit. If we do not soon release our hold on this storm—that is, allow it to resume its normal movement—it may simply decide not to move. I refer, as some of you will recognize, to the 'Megastorm' hypothesis." The Professor's voice was gradually increasing in volume. "This conceptualization asserts that when regions of cyclonic or anticyclonic circulation—that is, centers of low or high pressure—attain a certain critical durability, they may become semipermanent, immobile features of the troposphere, and thereby interrupt for an indefinite period the normal variability of local climatic regimes, most particularly in continental areas of the middle latitudes."

Vice President Lindemann offered a question. "Professor Uriah, has a Megastorm situation ever actually occurred?"

"Not historically, but some may have obtained during glacial maxima when zones of high pressure were fixed over the continental icecaps, blocking and displacing the storm tracks. Cyclones may at times have become 'trapped' or stalled. The so-called 'pluvial' climates characterized by inordinate precipitation provide a possible example. They contributed to the formation of vast Ice Age lakes in the intermountain west of North America. The Great Salt Lake is a remnant."

Professor Uriah concluded, "Unless the Great American Blizzard abates or is terminated very soon, there exists the indeterminate but finite probability that it will pass an unknown point of no return, a point or stage beyond which it would become self-generating and act as a brake on the west-to-east flow of weather waves around the northern hemisphere."

Defense Secretary Norris looked up at the giant scientist and raised his hand, as though he were a student in class. "That's a chilling scenario, Professor Uriah, but is there any hard evidence?"

"*Hard* evidence?"

"You know, firm . . . solid," he explained.

"The Megastorm concept is a hypothesis. There is some indication that the braking effect it predicts has, in fact, already begun. Since Thursday, storm migration across the United States has slowed dramatically. A low-pressure center over the Texas panhandle has apparently stalled and is now developing into one of the worst blizzards on the southern Plains in a good many years." Dr. Uriah swallowed some water.

"I repeat, if the normal eastward migration of northern-hemispheric weather does not soon resume, it may not resume at all—for a catastrophically long time." The professor's powerful voice boomed, reverberating with drama. "Other storm systems around the world may be expected to stall and intensify as our Great Blizzard has done. This will be most noticeable in localities such as western Europe, where severe winter storms are unusual. For example, in the

253

Paris basin, which is approximately two wavelengths east of this storm.

"But, *but,* ladies and gentlemen, of even greater significance to the furture of mankind are the implications of the 'Snowblitz' hypothesis."

" 'Snow*blitz?*' " Secretary Kroner repeated uncertainly.

"That is the accepted designation," Professor Uriah continued. "It applies to a legitimate hypothesis of comparatively recent formulation which holds that a period of extensive glaciation on the earth's continents may be initiated in a very short interval of time—that is, in a few days, a week, a month, or a year—rather than developing gradually over the much longer periods of centuries and millennia, as has been generally accepted by physical scientists since the middle of the nineteenth century.

"Now," the venerable scientist smoothed his mane of white hair, "if an anchoring effect should take hold, then the growth of the snowfield above our heads and similar accumulations elsewhere would inevitably lead to the development of larger and larger snowfields, then enlarging icecap cores, and finally to continental glaciers themselves." The professor's voice trembled with emotion as his arms swept outward and upward. "We may be dealing with Nature in revolution!" He paused for impact.

Secretary Norris was waving his hand again. "Ahh, Dr. Uriah . . . ?" he began timidly.

"Sir?"

"Does this mean that the Blizzard might lead to a new Ice Age?"

"It does *indeed.*" Professor Uriah's eyebrows arched over exaggeratedly wide, owl-like eyes. "In a relatively short time, this circumstance could cool the northern climates the few degrees necessary to initiate the next glacial stage of the Pleistocene Epoch. Thus, if we are unable to terminate the Blizzard before it reaches and passes the critical point of self-generation—which *could* be this exact moment," his voice rose as he thrust his right index finger toward the ceiling, "then we may face first Megastorm, then Snowblitz, and then . . ." His voice suddenly softened almost to a whisper. "And then the very Ice Age itself."

26

~~~~~~

WASHINGTON NATIONAL AIRPORT:
   11:00 AM, SUNDAY, DECEMBER 24

TEMPERATURE: 19°F

BAROMETER: 27.94″ (FALLING)

WIND: NE 70–95 MPH

SNOW DEPTH: 11′ (DRIFTS OVER 8 STORIES)

FORECAST: SNOW ENDING TODAY,
   CLEARING AND COLDER TONIGHT

"What?" blurted Matthew Rodek into the miniature microphone curving down from his headset. A pause. "All right. I guess that's it." He turned to Duncan

Smith, who was about to sit down at his side within the abyssal bathyscaphe *Nessie*. "No reprieve. We're goin' down." His companion simply nodded. Both men were tired.

Smith began the laborious procedure of making the many equipment tests that were itemized on their lengthy checklist. He had done it numerous times in training, but never as part of an actual mission under emergency conditions. Although the interior of the submersible was relatively cool, he was sweating profusely.

Rodek was annoyed, not nervous. He disliked the inconvenience of his situation. The ordeal had passed the point of being an adventurous way of making money. And he disliked Duncan Smith. He would have preferred sitting home in Chicago, watching the blizzard news on television. He turned to inspect the electronic video system; the one-by-two-foot screen would show a television projection image of the view seen by a rotatable camera mounted in solid epoxy just forward of the hatch.

Nine minutes later, *Nessie* was released by the remote-controlled derricks on the deck of the submerged *Leopard Shark*. She started her descent of four thousand meters to the bottom of the Atlantic.

As it had been almost continuously for forty-eight hours, the Cabinet Room in the White House was crowded and tense. Hurricane-force winds wailed incessantly beyond its walls. Live transmissions from *Nessie* via *Narwhal* were statically bursting from portable speakers propped against the long wall opposite the windows, "Four hundred fathoms," reported Matthew Rodek in his nasal Midwestern drone.

"Nine seconds west-southwest of plumb beneath *Narwhal*. Cabin pressure stable."

Hands clasped behind him, the President was pacing back and forth near the head of the elliptical table. Professor Uriah sat in the far right-hand corner, his great size dwarfing the chair. Several seats to his left, Joni Dubin was taking notes on a stenographer's pad—verbatim notes of all transmissions. Two White House tape recorders were in operation, but she was unsure of the future availability of the tapes and was determined to have her own record. She had filled five such notebooks in the past two days.

Facing her from across the table was Paul Garfield. Wearing a headset with an attached microphone, he too was making notes on a pad. The communications equipment had been wired up from the Situation Room beneath the White House, where direct transmissions from both *Narwhal* and Low Blow Operations Control were being received. Matthew Rodek's voice came again: "Six hundred fathoms. Four seconds due east of plumb beneath *Narwhal*. Cabin pressure stable."

Inside the descending submersible, Duncan Smith turned to Rodek. "Do you know Paul Garfield well?"

"Nah. Not really. I met him a few times when this project got started. He was in charge of it then. Seemed like a pretty good sort. If anybody can figure out how to reactivate the reactor controls, he should be able to."

"My God, can you imagine what might happen if we can't?"

"Hell," Rodek shrugged, "we'd just as well stay down there."

258

"Why was Garfield fired?" Smith inquired.

"He wasn't. He quit."

"That's not what I heard."

"Well, that's what happened," Rodek replied. "He didn't go for that Cuban application. Zimber took it out of his hands, so he quit."

"What Cuban application?"

"Oh, well now. That's a long story. Anyway, it was a cheat. Wasn't supposed to happen. Zimber was playing his own secret war game. That son of a bitch." Rodek frowned. "I used to think he was hot shit—till I found out he was gonna blow us up with that mine." Rodek reached for the rudder control. "Hey, we're gettin' too far off signal."

"Eight hundred fathoms," noised from the speaker in the Cabinet Room "Seven seconds of arc east-northeast of plumb beneath *Narwhal*. Cabin pressure stable. Cabin temperature twenty-nine. Gettin' a little warm. Receiving Low Blow location signal—weak." Rodek cut out. The clock read 11:41.

Beyond the stage of expressing their doubts and concerns during this critical vigil, people were engaging in nervous, disjointed small talk. Although fatigued and unshaven, Professor Uriah retained his dignity and formal manner of speaking. He glanced at Albert Kaufman. "I know that the technology is so highly developed that construction is now a simple matter, but nonetheless it amazes me that an undersea ship can withstand such extremely high pressures as those to which this submersible will be subjected."

"Aw, hell, Professor," interrupted the Chief of Naval Operations, "old Rodek took her down to five

259

thousand meters when we brought up part of the Soviet sub."

"What amazes me," commented the Secretary of State, "is that radio tramsmissions are possible through so much water."

Albert Kaufman responded, "Actually the signals are clearer and travel more rapidly, provided there is no thermal inversion layer to interfere. And in this case, they're descending through an upward current so that all inversions are disrupted. Theoretically, you could send an underwater signal around the entire earth—and without the atmospheric interference caused by solar radiation."

The President glanced at his watch. "It shouldn't be much longer." His words were lost in the screaming of the wind.

Facing toward *Nessie*'s stern, Duncan Smith was adjusting the radio receiver system. They were homing in on the location signal from the master reactor. Rodek was operating the submersible's guidance controls, his eyes focused on the display of guages and digital meters before him. He was beginning to gain more respect for his colleague's competence. But, as was his nature, he was still very abrupt. It was time for another report.

"One thousand fathoms," barked Matthew. "Two and a half seconds north of plumb beneath *Narwhal*. Four thousand yards northwest of plumb above Low Blow signal. Cabin pressure stable. Cabin temp thirty-one."

Slowly they sank through another thousand meters. Rodek and Smith were both sweating freely now. "Better get on the screen, Smith. We're pretty close."

The report from fifteen hundred fathoms had just come in. Everyone in the Cabinet Room was listening intently. The President sat down next to Paul Garfield.

"Approaching master reactor," Rodek's voice reported.

"Rodek, this is Garfield. Try STOP command."

There was a long pause, then Rodek's voice came through static: "STOP command, still no response."

Professor Uriah began to speak. "My hope is that—"

"SLOW DOWN command," Paul interrupted.

Another pause, and: "SLOW DOWN command. No response. Two thousand and eight fathoms. Three fathoms from fine-sand bottom. Spotlights functioning. Reactor image on screen. Are you receiving? Are you receiving?"

"*Narhwal* yes, White House yes," confirmed the voice of Arnold Berger from the Situation Room. An image slowly took shape on the closed-circuit television screen in the Cabinet Room. There it was: round and black, but indistinct and very snowy.

Rodek guided *Nessie* closer to the reactor. Then the submersible slowed and stopped. "We need to get closer to attach the contact transmitter," said Smith, who was hunched over the video screen.

"Fuckin' thing's stalled," Rodek cursed as he pressed the START button.

"What's wrong?" asked Garfield's voice in the earphones.

"Can't use the contact transmitter yet 'cause we're stalled," Rodek replied. Again he pushed START.

"A regular radio command at the close range

should work unless there's severe damage," Paul commented.

"Son of a bitch, we'd better get this mother restarted," growled Matthew "Ah, there she comes."

"What?" Garfield asked.

"We got it restarted. Thank God, we got her restarted!" shouted a very relieved Matthew Rodek.

"Listen, Rodek. That gives me an idea," Paul announced. "Try the RESTART command on the reactor, then a STOP."

Rodek complied, and there was an interruption in the reactor engines. An interruption! "We got a short break, but they started up again," he said excitedly.

"Good. Now try putting both those commands on memory-hold and releasing them simultaneously," Garfield suggested.

Rodek carefully punched the command combinations and the hold buttons. Then he released both at once. The reactor engines stopped. "They've stopped," he yelled. "The reactor engines have stopped!"

There was stand-up cheering in the Cabinet Room. The President applauded and called for a steward. Joni Dubin dropped her pad and ran around the table to embrace Paul. General Wilcox stooped over and took a pint of bourbon from his briefcase. Spirits were so high and the relief so great that the wind outside and the water-stained plaster overhead were temporarily forgotten.

Professor Uriah, however, remained seated, staring at the windows. He did not join in the celebration. Wet with perspiration, the left side of his face was twitching uncontrollably. He wanted to be alone.

Lifting his great bulk, he moved toward the door as the President was accepting the Scotch-in-a-brandy-glass that he had ordered. The Chief Executive lofted the snifter and offered a toast. "To the total success of this mission."

Turning in the doorway, Professor Uriah cautioned, "Mr. President, I should like with all the passion of my heart to join in your toast, but I cannot. For the accomplishment which you celebrate is but a tentative and frighteningly uncertain initial step. It merely permits us to wait for the greater answer. The terrible test is now beginning. Have we ceased our interference in time?"

He turned to go but looked back once more. "I may comment that the eve of the Messiah's birth is an appropriate time for waiting." The hulking cosmologist went out.

27

WASHINGTON NATIONAL AIRPORT:
6:00 PM, SUNDAY, DECEMBER 24

TEMPERATURE: 18°F

BAROMETER: 27.81″ (FALLING)

WIND: NE 75–105 MPH

SNOW DEPTH: 12′ (DRIFTS OVER 10 STORIES)

FORECAST: SNOW ENDING TONIGHT,
CLEARING AND COLD TOMORROW

A tired André Geler was in the midst of a report on storm conditions. He could barely be heard in the Cabinet Room above the sound of the wind. ". . . and the wind is now continually at or above

264

minimum hurricane force all along the coast from Richmond, Virginia, north to Portland, Maine. Near the center of the storm, winds exceed two hundred miles per hour—the most extreme ever recorded for a hurricane or typhoon. Approaching tornadic velocity. The barometric pressure at sea level is also now lower than any ever recorded—even for the eyes of the most severe hurricanes. Down near twenty-seven and a half inches of mercury. Approaching tornadic pressure.

"As you know, we are awaiting an update on these data from *Narwhal* and our hurricane planes to see whether there has finally been a change in the earlier trends. We have received no new data for several hours." The Director of NOAA waited for questions. There were none, so he sat down. The room was much less crowded than before; about half of the chairs were occupied.

Outside, snowdrifts had grown into huge, elongate dunes. Some were more than one hundred feet high. They covered, actually buried, buildings of four, six, even ten stories. Recent reports of the blizzard centered in the Texas panhandle had described the paralysis of eastern Colorado, Kansas, and Oklahoma; it was now a record-breaking snowstorm for that region.

No one was talking in the Cabinet Room. Fatigued and frustrated, members of the National Security Council sat and waited. CIA Director Satin was asleep. Professor Uriah had returned and was studying a journal. Reports on emergency conditions in various parts of the Northeast periodically spurted from speakers. Joni Dubin and Paul Garfield were sitting against the long wall opposite the windows. She was leaning on his shoulder with her eyes closed. David Bradford had returned to his office.

The President rose from his chair at the head of the table and motioned for Herbert Salisbury. "Herb, if things haven't turned the corner in the next report, then we'd better put Operation Exodus into—"

His remarks were interrupted by a sputtering transmission from Captain Nansen on the U.S.S. *Narwhal;* ". . . barometer still falling off, going off . . ." The message was broken by static, then ceased altogether. An uncertain groan rippled throughout the room.

A large television-projection screen at the far end of the table was displaying a live satellite image of the Blizzard, a huge, shimmering white spiral. It reminded Joni of a galaxy. Professor Uriah was gazing at the thing as if hypnotized, rocking slowly back and forth in his chair, nodding with his entire body. Joni became conscious of the word that dominated his mind: Megastorm. *Megastorm. MEGASTORM.* How can he not blink, she wondered.

The vibrations began as the President and Herbert Salisbury were walking toward the door. Shaking, then jostling, jolting from above. Thomas Jefferson's portrait fell to the floor. *Violent crashing.* "What in hell?" cried the President. Paul and Joni held each other tightly as they looked up at the rupturing ceiling.

The West Wing of the White House was breaking down under the mass of an eighty-five-foot snowdrift.

28

CHARLES DE GAULLE INTERNATIONAL
  AIRPORT: 1:00 AM, MONDAY, DECEMBER 25

TEMPERATURE: 31°F

BAROMETER: 29.89″ (FALLING)

WIND: E 12–17 MPH

PRECIPITATION: NONE

FORECAST: CLEARING AND COLD TODAY,
  WARMER TOMORROW

A purring Burmese cat, tail straight up, glided under
the Christmas tree and rubbed against the trunk. It
vaulted in fright when the tree lights lit. As the
family began singing "Il Est Né le Divin Enfant,"

267

the cat moved quickly to the corner behind the tree. The song was followed by a happy mixture of talking and laughter and toasts for the holiday. "Joyeux Noël! Joyeux Noël!"

"C'est merveilleux d'avoir la famille rassemblée, n'est-ce pas?" smiled Grandmother.

"Oui, mais comment peut-on être complètement heureux tout en se rendant compte de la catastrophe aux États-Unis?" asked her daughter, lamenting the disaster in America.

During a lull in the festivities, the boy's voice was finally heard. It repeated, "Regardez. Regardez. Il neige! Il *neige!*"

One by one they gathered at the window. The street lamps below shone in broad arcs of settling feathers. It was snowing. It was actually snowing. Unusual enough in Paris, but on Christmas morning: "Que c'est extraordinaire! Que c'est belle!" There were cheers and applause.

On the sidewalk beneath them, an old man wearing a black cape was shuffling along with the aid of a walking stick. Abruptly he stopped to wipe his eye. Reaching for his handkerchief, he squinted up at the cloud-laden sky. In the distance, Notre Dame was fading from view behind the falling white flakes.

There ariseth a little cloud out of the sea, like a man's hand.

—I Kings 18:44

Dell Bestsellers

the sizzling novel of a 20th century tycoon
by Eddie Constantine, author
of _The God Player_

In 1939, in Nazi-run France, the penniless young son of a village whore began his odyssey of ambition . . .

Within a decade, Charles de Belmont was one of the richest financiers in the world. He'd loved the most beautiful, the choicest women. And controlled the most powerful—and dangerous—men.

He'd learned to play THE ODDS.

Dell $2.25

A NOVEL
by Stirling Silliphant

★ ★ ★ ★ ★ ★ ★ ★ ★ ★ ★ ★ ★ ★ ★ ★ ★ ★ ★ ★

In December of 1941, the Hawaiian island of Oahu seemed as close to Eden as any place, until the massive military destruction in the tropical paradise shook the world! PEARL focuses on six people who are permanently scarred by the event· a U.S. Army colonel and his wife, a woman obstetrician and an Army captain, and a Japanese-American girl and a young Navy flier It is a novel of shattered lives, dreams and innocence, in one of the most crushing events in U.S. history—the bombing of Pearl Harbor!

Now a Spectacular ABC-TV movie!

A Dell Book · $2.50